MIA UNARMED

Praise for "Mia Unarmed"

Mia Unarmed

Kathleen McElligott

Contents

"Resilience is accepting your new reality, even if it's less good than the one you had before. You can fight it, you can do nothing but scream about what you've lost, or you can accept that and try to put together something that's good."

- Elizabeth Edwards, Attorney, Author, Activist.

Part I

1

I opened my eyes and stared up at the ceiling for a few seconds before I remembered that it was my birthday. Not just any birthday, my thirteenth birthday. I was excited and nervous, too. Still in my pj's, I made my way downstairs. Mother was mixing the batter for my birthday cake, coconut crème with freshly shredded coconut on top, my favorite. I hungrily eyed the beaters as she lifted them from the bowl.

"Oh, go ahead if you must," she said as she offered me one. I savored the sweet creaminess, blissfully humming with delight.

"It's super fattening, but it is your special day." Like she had to remind me, about the fat part.

"Thanks, Mother," I said, rolling my eyes and smirking as only a newly minted teenager can, "for reminding me that I'm fat. On my birthday, no less. You couldn't let it go for once."

"You're not fat, you're still growing," Mother offered. But I know it bothers her. More than me.

She made the final decision on all my clothes. She'd make comments like "Those slacks are very slimming," so I guessed that everything else made me look like a cow. I chose a pink tunic over black leggings with a rhinestone-studded belt that was supposed to give the impression of a waistline.

Mother was always put together: capris with a matching knit top, her hair perfectly styled, thanks to a weekly visit to the salon, jewelry tastefully understated. How could I compete with *that?* Not that I was trying.

My image stared back at me as I brushed my teeth—shoulder length brown hair that was due for a shampoo and grey eyes. Boring! I forgot to mention that I have a slight bump on the bridge of my nose from when I slipped on a patch of ice and face-planted as I was waiting in line to careen down the toboggan run. I liked pushing limits, taking chances, but so far I hadn't had much of an opportunity.

The hallway is always chaos in the morning, Kids slamming their lockers shut after getting what they needed, greetings shouted across the hall, students running to make it to class on time. I held my breath as I walked down the hall to my locker. I was hoping I would find a birthday banner or paper flowers. No such luck. Instead, a knot of girls giggled and pointed at me as I approached my sadly unadorned locker. Chloe, with her blonde hair and cute, upturned nose smiled sympathetically but instead of a birthday greeting she said sarcastically, "You know, Mia, if you weren't so...well there's no other way to say it...fat, and if you got your nose fixed you might have some friends." Chloe's minions glanced furtively from me to Chloe and giggled conspiratorially, waiting for me to respond.

My eyes stung with unshed tears but instead of crying, I fired back.

"You're thick as a brick, Chloe. Sorry, but there's no other way to say it. If you spent more time studying and less time harassing me and chasing boys, you might avoid summer school again this year!" No way was I going to let Chloe dis me in front of the school's most notorious mean girls on my thirteenth birthday!

~

It was true, though. Chloe couldn't solve a simple math problem if her life depended on it. That's the thing—I'm smart. Other girls in my class were too, but they went out of their way to hide it, running in packs and giggling like morons when boys were around. As far as I'm concerned, the boys at my school, Kennison Junior High, were nose-picking troglodytes, unworthy of a second glance or a second thought.Ugh! I couldn't care less about being popular. It was a big deal for Mother, though, who would stop at nothing to hoist me up the social ladder. Last year she threw a big Halloween party and invited everyone in the class. She was disappointed when only a handful of kids showed up—and they weren't the popular crowd.

While we sat around on the basement floor eating chocolate cupcakes with cream cheese frosting (Yum!) and orange sprinkles, Sam, a nerdy but sweet brainiac explained the finer points of the evolution of All Hallows Eve. We even turned off the lights and told ghost stories that weren't the least bit scary.

In the weeks leading up to my birthday I hinted that I wanted an easel and painting kit. Everyone says I'm the best artist in the class. I got to draw a get-well card for everyone to sign when someone in the class is sick.

I got a handgun instead, wrapped in tissue paper and nestled in a pink satin pouch. A Glock 42, one of the lightest and smallest handguns. Fully loaded, it weighed a little over a pound. I shouldn't have been surprised. Everyone in Kennison received a gun on their thirteenth birthday. It was a rite of passage—expected, endorsed, encouraged, even.

~

Guns were everywhere in Kennison and shootings were an everyday occurrence. Each new mayor promised to eliminate gun violence as a top priority, but with conceal carry legal for anyone age thirteen and over and the number of weapons available, it was impossible. What began as an attempt to ensure everyone's safety meant that in reality, no one was safe. Children were especially vulnerable. Gunshot was the leading cause of death for children in Kennison and throughout the Autonomous States, but nobody wanted to talk about it until the next school shooting. The government's solution was *more guns,* not less.

People who refused to weaponize were referred to as *'The Unarmed.'* They were considered the radical fringe and viewed with suspicion. The Unarmed were easy to track because the gun registration system was computerized, unlike the sketchy handwritten records of earlier administrations. In the past, gun registration was viewed as an obstacle to gun ownership. Under the current administration, tight gun registration records promoted legal gun ownership. "An armed society is a safe society," was the national slogan, but the number of gun-related deaths, both intentional and accidental, proved otherwise.

~

Eighth grade flew by in a blur. I did what I always did, got good grades and kept out of trouble. I kept to myself and tried to steer clear of Chloe and her friends whenever possible, but it wasn't always possible. Especially in PE where we were all grouped together regardless of academic performance. I tried to change into my gym uniform as quickly as possible, but somehow Chloe always found me just as I was pulling up my shorts. Animal sounds were her specialty, grunting like a pig or mooing like a cow.

"Drop dead, Chloe." I said as I hurried out to the gym.

"Oh, Mia. You don't really mean that, do you? You know I was just kidding." Chloe said in a fake syrupy sweet voice.

"Get out of my way," I said as I pushed past her. She stood there with her hands on her hips, laughing.

As graduation approached, I asked Dad to help me with my speech. I was a shoo-in to represent my class since I had the highest GPA and no discipline demerits. Prying him away from his computer was no easy task. For as long as I could remember he worked from home, glued to his computer. I had no idea what he did. When I asked, he brushed me off reminding me that we lived a comfortable life in a comfortable home with plenty to eat and nice clothes to wear. End of story. I still wondered, though. He read my speech, made a few changes and said that before I began speaking I should take a deep breath and imagine the audience in their underwear. Not *I'm so proud of you, good job,* or whatever. Imagining my classmates and teachers in their underwear was the extent of his advice.

On graduation day I took a breath, exhaled, and stifled a laugh as I imagined Mr. Slocum in his boxers. I delivered my speech about finding our path in life as responsible citizens of our country and the world. My parents, Nina and Dick, gazed adoringly from the front row of folding chairs in the gym. I breathed a sigh of relief as I exited the stage.

After the ceremony my parents informed me that I would be attending New Hope Academy, an elite girls' school in Kennison. I wasn't consulted. *They* thought it was the best choice for me. "You'll have many opportunities there," Mother said with a hopeful gleam in her eye, no doubt thinking about my busy social life and acceptance into first-rate universities. One bright spot was that students at New Hope wore uniforms: a white blouse, navy blazer, khaki skirt or slacks. At least Mother couldn't dictate what I wore to school anymore. Most girls I talked to hated the idea of uniforms. I welcomed it. Everyone dressed the same from top to bottom meant no one stood out, we were all equals. I could roll out of bed without wasting time deciding what to wear.

The first semester at New Hope was a game changer for me. At Kennison Elementary I excelled with little effort. New Hope was different. Academic expectations were high. Parents demanded a return on their hefty private school investment. No boys meant fierce competition among the girls. My classmates weren't shy about striving for the highest GPA. The curriculum was heavy on problem solving and essay writing. I hated writing essays, but I became good at it out of necessity. I considered it a challenge. At New Hope we were encouraged to think for ourselves, not just regurgitate facts.

Natalie, a classmate whom I'd noticed from day one, was cute and funny, a true brainiac and a bit of a rebel as well. She rolled the waistband of her skirt to shorten it, unconcerned about demerits. We were the only two to get an "A" on our first Math quiz. Unlike me, Natalie was confident and had a gaggle of friends. She called to me after class one day. I stopped and looked around. "Me?" *She means me!*

"Hi, I'm Natalie. We both got an "A" on the quiz, but don't get too cocky. Kids don't like it when you raise the curve. My sister graduated two years ago—she warned me about it," she said, smiling widely, not trying to hide her braces. "Are you taking Mr. Helm's Social Justice class? You definitely should. We get to go on a field trip later in the year."

"I am," I said, standing up taller and sucking in my belly, something Mother always nagged me about. I'd made a friend! Natalie giggled. Her freckles darkened against her pale cheeks. She smelled faintly of peppermint. I adored her immediately.

~

Mr. Helm was tall and blond. His nose was slightly crooked which only added to his appeal. Did he break it in a brawl or motorcycle crash, I wondered. His blue eyes and white teeth made it difficult to concentrate. *Do I have a crush on Mr. Helm?* I glanced at my classmates. Clearly, I wasn't the only one.

Handsome as he was, as a teacher he was no pushover. Our first assignment was a five-hundred-word essay explaining how carrying a gun reduces violence. *What?* My head ached. Carrying a weapon was expected, it's what you did. Those who refused were Unarmed and considered suspicious radicals. I felt uneasy about the assignment but I wanted to please Mr. Helm. I could easily churn out an 'A' paper, but I sensed that he wanted something more than a rote answer.

I lay awake at night thinking about the assignment. I stared at the ceiling while I petted Tinker, my Tabby. It was the first time I had to explain something that I took for granted, that we all took for granted. Being armed made everyone equal so why risk getting shot? Still, there continued to be gun violence—armed robberies, drive-by, road rage and school shootings made the news every day. It seemed like everyone was numb to the violence and nobody had a solution. Some even thought that the solution was *more* guns.

Once, on a train trip downtown with Mother we encountered a grungy teenager blasting his music, glaring at anyone to defy him. No one said a word but the passengers were obviously uncomfortable. We sat silently while the noise bounced off the walls of the commuter car. The train was full so we couldn't move to another car. Mother, of course, was armed, yet we were at a standoff. She squeezed my hand, afraid to say anything even if it was only to ask him to turn down his music. So that was her solution, don't make waves, just sit quietly until we got off the train.

On the first day of Social Action Club, Mr. Helm invited anyone who was interested in joining to stay after school. I glanced over at Natalie. She smiled and gave a thumbs-up! I couldn't wait to be in a club with Natalie. After dismissal I stopped at my locker. Girls were changing into leggings and oversized sweatshirts with the school logo: a yellow sun with rays of light shining down on the school's name. They looked so stylish and comfy. I made a mental note to get one of those sweatshirts and wear leggings to the next meeting. I had so much to learn if I wanted to fit in.

Girls chatted and joked as we waited for Mr. Helm to start the meeting. Natalie knew everyone and introduced me. I was floating on a cloud. For the first time in my life, I felt like I belonged.

Mr. Helm welcomed us then loosened his tie and rolled up his sleeves revealing tanned, muscular arms. "Well ladies, I'm off the clock now so I'll ditch this." With that he removed his tie and stuffed it in a desk drawer. "You're here because you're interested in social action." We nodded in agreement.

"Any thoughts?" he asked.

Natalie was the first to speak. "My sister went on a field trip with Social Action a few years ago and met *homeless* people!" She glanced around the room gauging our reaction to this revelation.

Some shifted in their seats, others made muffled comments to their neighbor.

"Yes, ladies," (he always called us ladies) "even in Kennison, there is a homeless population. They're not considered a threat, so you don't hear or read much about them, but they're out there, believe me. We'll not only discuss what it's like to be homeless, but we'll be collecting winter clothing that we will distribute to them, so start going through your closets now."

He went on to talk about something called *demographics* that made it sound like we were darn lucky to be living where we did, in a place with high income, good schools, parks, resources and so on. I never thought of Kennison that way before. He said that because we had all these advantages, we needed to share our good fortune with others. Thus, the Social Action Club.

When I got home Mother asked about the meeting, what it was about and who was in it. I worried that she wouldn't let me go on the field trip so I only told her we were collecting coats and jackets for the homeless. I was basking in the glow of acceptance by Natalie and her friends and didn't want Mother to ruin it. "Good, I'll go through my closet and get rid of some outdated but perfectly serviceable items." That was *so* Mother. Clear her closet to make room for new stuff. Unlike me she was all about shopping for new clothes.

Being homeless was something I couldn't wrap my head around. It was October. The days were still warm and I slept with the windows open. The trees were a riot of color and a whiff of woodsmoke hung in the air. Soon the temperature would drop followed by grey skies, and eventually sleet and snow. Where do the homeless go in winter, I wondered. I decided to donate a puffy down jacket that made me look like a pink marshmallow. And some blankets. We had so many we'd never miss them.

In class the next day Mr. Helm pointed to the clear plastic box mounted on the wall behind his desk. "What is this, ladies, and why is it there?" he asked no one in particular.

"It's a gun to protect us from an intruder," I offered, without raising my hand. Didn't everyone know that?

"Thank you, Mia."

"Think about this, ladies. Why do we need a loaded gun in our classroom? In every classroom in this school? In every classroom in this country?" We sat silently for a few moments, shifting uneasily in our seats.

After an uncomfortable silence Natalie responded in a quiet voice, "Kids and teachers are easy targets. We need protection."

"This is a school. A place of learning and ideas. If an intruder suddenly stormed in here, would you defend your classmates and yourself? You've all armed." We all froze.

Suddenly he slammed his fist on the desk. I gasped and bolted upright in my seat.

"Protecting yourselves and your classmates against intruders is not your responsibility, ladies. Society and our government have failed you!"

In The Autonomous States, Weapons Defense was a mandatory class for all students. Every classroom was equipped with a Plexiglass gun box, like a fire alarm. If "Code Red" was announced over the intercom, the teacher opened the lid and removed the loaded gun. The box was in the same location in every classroom and positioned within reach of the students in that grade. When opened, a silent alarm and a video camera were activated sending live feed to the office and the local police. The video was supposed to help identify the shooter and his location.

~

Two weeks before winter break Mr. Helm made the announcement we had all been waiting for.

"Ladies, next week we're going on a field trip, one that will heighten your awareness of social inequity. We're going to visit a homeless camp to distribute the clothing and blankets you've collected."

We clapped and hooted. We're going to Kennison with Mr. Helm!

~

A milky December sun neared the horizon as our group of twenty waited in the school parking lot for the bus. Mother had reluctantly signed my permission slip. "Are you sure it's safe?" I assured her it was and that Natalie's sister had gone a few years ago. I checked that my Glock was loaded and the safety engaged and stashed it in my backpack. As Mr. Helm walked toward the group, someone called out to him, "Where's *your* weapon, Mr. Helm?" I wasn't prepared for his response.

"I don't carry a weapon, ladies. I'm unarmed." We stared wide-eyed, shocked that our teacher was unarmed.

"I lost my twin brother five years ago. He was talking to some friends on the quad on a warm spring day. He was armed, of course. But he didn't stand a chance against a drive-by shooter with an assault weapon who mowed down my brother and three of his friends. I'll never get that bloody image out of my head."

I turned to Natalie. She shrugged, "So what? Mr. Helm is a badass!" she said with a defiant gleam in her eye.

"You knew, didn't you?" I demanded. "Why didn't you tell me?"

"Because I knew you wouldn't go if you found out Mr. Helm was unarmed."

"But Natalie, what if something happens? He can't defend us. If I get shot my mother will kill me!"

"I'm armed and so are you, right? We can take care of ourselves!" She snapped, her freckles darkening. *Can we?* I wondered.

"But I never thought I'd have to use it. Just carry it like we're supposed to!"

"What are you going to do, call your mother to come and get you?" she challenged, her green eyes like molten emeralds.

"No, I'm getting on that bus." I'd prove I was just as brave as Natalie.

On the way into the city, I felt the outline of the Glock in the bottom of my backpack. A flock of deranged birds flapped around in my stomach but there was no turning back now. We were on our way. It was up to us to defend ourselves. Natalie assured me that everything would be alright and reminded me that nothing had happened to her sister. But that was then and this was now.

The last traces of daylight were fading as the bus exited the highway and made its way through a run-down neighborhood with boarded-up windows and streets littered with broken glass and fast-food wrappers. The bus pulled into a weedy vacant lot next to a crumbling viaduct and trembled to a stop. Mr. Helm stood up and turned toward us. I held my breath in anticipation. I thought about staying in the bus, hiding behind a seat, but Natalie elbowed me to pay attention.

"We need to stick together, ladies. Do not go off on your own. We're here to give the items we've collected to the homeless people living here. You'll each get a large plastic bag with a blanket, a coat and a pair of new socks for your client. There will be no haggling over color or size. The clients can trade with each other after we leave."

Clients, they're called clients, I mused.

I slipped the straps of my backpack over my shoulders and fingered the outline of my Glock for reassurance. As we exited the bus Mr. Helm handed each of us a bag. We huddled around him like a gaggle of newly hatched chicks and headed toward the underpass.

A figure, slightly built, dressed in a black hoodie and jeans emerged from the crumbling viaduct and approached our group. Mr. Helm extended his hand, "Juan, it's good to see you. I brought some new recruits." Juan nodded and motioned for us to follow him beneath an archway with '1929' inscribed in a block of pitted concrete at the peak of the underpass. A steady stream of cars and trucks zoomed overhead, causing the ancient structure to vibrate. I was terrified that it might collapse while we were inside, but I kept it to myself. I didn't want more grief from Natalie. Moisture seeped through spidery cracks in the graffiti covered walls.

The smell smacked me in the face, worse than sweaty gym clothes stashed in a locker for weeks, or the outhouse at summer camp without the pine disinfectant. I tried to breathe through my mouth to keep from gagging. My eyes slowly adjusted to the gloom. People were bundled in layers of mismatched clothing and raggedy blankets, sitting or lying on pallets of flattened cardboard. It was difficult to tell men from women. Mr. Helm approached a lone figure.

"Hi, my name is David. How are you doing? You keeping warm?"

Even in the dim light I could see an unshaven man, his clothes were worn and dirty. The whites of his eyes shone cartoon-like in the darkness. "I'm doin' okay. It ain't so cold—not yet anyways." His smile was like a Halloween jack-o-lantern with missing teeth.

"Here's a blanket and jacket for the serious cold." Mr. Helm held out the bag. The man grabbed it and held it to his chest as if someone might snatch it.

"Yeah, thanks." the man mumbled.

Now it was our turn to find a client. I walked deeper into the cavern, taking baby steps, careful not to step on anyone. Someone waved me over. I walked slowly, wondering what to say. She was a scarecrow of a woman, her gaunt eyes peering out from beneath an oversized hoodie. Strands of straw-like hair poked out at odd angles. She motioned for me to sit.

"I'm Minnie," she said in a raspy voice.

"I'm Mia." There were so many questions I wanted to ask like, *how did you end up here, where's your family, how do you brush your teeth, and more importantly, where do you go to the toilet?* But Mr. Helm lectured us about respecting our clients' privacy. No matter how they got here, we were here to help, not judge. "I brought you a coat and blanket." I handed her the bag and she peered inside. She needed so much more than what was inside that bag. I was sad and embarrassed that I didn't have more to give. It was a start, though. I thought about taking her home with me, feeding her and letting her soak in our bathtub. Mother would go ballistic. I'd have to do it when she wasn't home. But for now, all I had to offer was a coat, blanket and men's athletic socks.

Then Minnie did something unexpected, she reached out and touched my hand with her bony fingers that poked out from fingerless gloves. "Thank you, Mia." We sat silently for a few seconds. "Would you like some crackers?" she asked, offering me a packet of Saltines, the kind you get with soup at a restaurant. They were all she had to eat. That really got to me.

I shook my head. In the corner of my eye, I saw Mr. Helm motioning that it was time to leave. As I said good-bye she clutched my hand, "You are an angel, Mia. Don't forget about me. I'll look for you every day."

~

We sat silently on the bus, lost in thought, confident that what we had just seen could never happen to us. But strangely, what should have been a hopeless and depressing experience wasn't. Minnie saying that she would look for me every day weighed on me. It was a heavy burden for a thirteen-year-old knowing that someone depended on me to return.

Dad was waiting for me in the parking lot. "Well, how was it?" he asked as I slammed into the car, full of plans to save the world, one homeless person at a time.

"I never knew people lived like that. It was awful!" I said, while I buckled my seatbelt. "Why can't we help them, I mean *really* help them, not just once a year?" I stared out the window at the stately old homes in my neighborhood. Colored lights twinkled and evergreen boughs festooned porches and stairways. The glow from within promised warmth and shelter from the cold and dark. It was a million miles from the cold and dark of the homeless camp.

"Mia, I know it's hard to understand, but those people are drug addicts or alcoholics. They can't or don't want to live a normal life." He stroked his cleanly shaven chin as if he had a full beard, something he did when he was being serious.

Those people. It sounded cold coming from my father. Until now I believed every word he said, but now I began to wonder. A pang of disappointment swept over me. He clearly didn't understand. *It's not their fault*, I wanted to scream.

"The lady I met, her name was Minnie. She was nice. She said I was an angel and she wanted me to come back."

"Whoa. Not so fast. You went once. You saw what it's like. You're not going back."

End of story. It wasn't open for discussion. He wouldn't listen to my opinion. He was the same way when he and Mother argued. He'd shut her down like slamming a door. She'd sit in her chair in the living room and stew, her lips pressed into a thin line. Dad would retreat to his office, his face eerily illuminated behind his computer screen. No one spoke for hours. The next day the tension hung in the air like last night's fish dinner. Nothing, it seemed, was ever resolved.

During winter break I couldn't stop thinking about Minnie, how she touched my hand and asked me not to forget her. No chance of that. Her image lingered—her sour odor, her dull, brittle hair, fingernails gnawed to the quick. But her eyes were kind and her words sincere despite her hoarse voice. I knew that I would return, even after Dad said *no*. I would find a way.

I had so many questions. What had happened to Minnie to cause her to become homeless, where was her family? Did she have children—grandchildren? My own Grandma Dottie died when I was a little kid. I can still smell her perfume, Evening in Paris, from a blue bottle on her dresser. Sometimes I dabbed some behind my ears like I'd seen her do. Whenever we visited she'd put out a plate of cookies that I didn't like but I ate them because Mother would nudge me to take one, then another. No wonder I was chunky even as a little kid!

Seeing how people scrabbled to survive in the homeless camp under the viaduct opened my eyes to a world I never knew existed. It was unsettling and that night in my cozy bed I was grateful for my new friend, Natalie, my comfortable home, food to eat, warm clothes and Tinker, of course. Learning that Mr. Helm was Unarmed was another shock. I'd never had a teacher like him before, telling us that our government had failed us. Still, he should have told us from the beginning. Not that I liked carrying a firearm around in my backpack. I never thought I'd ever have to use it, but after meeting Minnie, alone and homeless, I realized that she was easy prey and there were probably many more like her.

Christmas in my house meant a quiet day. I'd known since I was five that Santa didn't bring the presents on Christmas morning. How could he? We didn't have a fireplace, and besides, how could he possibly deliver gifts to all the children in the world in one evening? It just wasn't feasible. I didn't tell my parents that I didn't believe to spare their feelings. On a positive note, I did get the painting kit and easel that I wanted.

I couldn't wait to get back to the homeless camp and Minnie. After Christmas Natalie and I lay across my bed planning how we'd bring food and clothes and books. Flashlights and batteries, too. I held Tinker on my lap, stroking behind her ears, her favorite place. She purred appreciatively and closed her eyes. Natalie was propped up on her elbow munching a candy bar.

"Neither of us can drive—my parents won't take us, and I have no idea how to get there on a bus or train. I wouldn't want to get lost in that neighborhood." I admitted.

"Here," Natalie said, offering me a stick from her KitKat. "It'll help you think."

"You know I shouldn't eat this," I said, quickly popping it into my mouth. "Everyone's out to sabotage my diet," I complained.

"Get over it! We've got more important things to worry about, like how to get to 1929." 1929 became our code word for the homeless camp in Kennison.

"I've got it!" Natalie bolted upright. "My sister Emma is home on break. She can drive us! It's settled." Leave it to Natalie to come up with a solution.

~

I told Mother I was spending the night at Natalie's. It wasn't a lie because I *would be* spending the night after we returned from our mission. I'd never lied to Mother before, except for the usual stuff like I'd finished my term paper when I'd barely started it or I'd cleaned my room when I hadn't. She'd never find out. I felt a twinge of guilt, though. I stuffed my pajamas into my backpack over cans of condensed soup, boxes of stuffing and mac and cheese. I waited at the front door until Emma and Natalie pulled up in their parents' minivan.

"Bye," I yelled as I was about to bolt out the door.

"Get back here, young lady," Mother commanded.

Busted! *How did she find out?*

"Aren't you forgetting something?" I stared at the ceiling shifting my weight. What was I forgetting?

"What's her parents' number—just in case?"

I scribbled the number on a scrap of paper, a quick peck on the cheek and I was out the door, breathing a sigh of relief.

"That was close," I said as I hoisted my backpack into the van and climbed in.

"What did you bring?" Natalie asked.

"Cans of soup and boxes of stuffing and mac and cheese."

"Duh, how's Minnie supposed to cook soup and stuffing?" She had a point, but it was all I could sneak out of the pantry without Mother getting suspicious. I asked Natalie if her parents knew where we were going.

"They think we're going to the movies."

"We'd better get our stories straight. What movie are we supposed to see?" I asked.

"A sci-fi film I saw advertised. No chance our parents would have seen it."

"Good call." I had to hand it to Natalie. She was way ahead of me in the deception game.

Emma, who had been mostly silent during the drive, took the exit that led to 1929. A tepid sun had already set. The neighborhood looked exceptionally lethal; abandoned storefronts with soaped windows, trash blowing everywhere, a skinny dog trotting along a cracked sidewalk. The outline of the viaduct lay ahead. I imagined a graveyard at midnight.

"I hate to park here," Emma said, avoiding a chunk of concrete, "but I guess there's no other place."

Unlike our first outing, no one came out to greet us. I was nervous. My palms began to sweat. Not a good sign. We were truly on our own, privileged kids from the good side of town. Natalie and I sidled up to Emma as we made our way under the arch. The rank odor greeted us.

I gulped a mouthful of air and held my breath as long as I could. My eyes adjusted to the gloom. I looked for Minnie but she wasn't where I had last seen her. A burly man wrapped in a blanket sitting cross-legged on a plastic tarp was in her spot.

"Excuse me, sir, have you seen Minnie? She's a friend of mine."

He stared through me with vacant eyes. Then a voice called out, "She's over at the other end."

"Thanks," I replied to the disembodied voice and made my way toward the opposite entrance, while Natalie and Emma handed out food and supplies.

I spotted a thin figure with tufts of unruly hair.

"Minnie?" I asked tentatively as I approached. Her eyes lit up as she stood to greet me.

"Mia? Is that you?" Minnie was sitting on a ragged blanket over layers of cardboard. A half-filled garbage bag was within arms' reach. "You came back!" She said in her scratchy voice. "I knew you would. I looked for you every day."

The thought made me sad and somehow unworthy of her trust. If it weren't for Emma, I wouldn't be here. For the first time in my life, I felt responsibility for someone other than myself. A bond was forming between us. She had counted on me and I didn't let her down.

I handed her the cans and boxes, apologizing that she had no way to heat the food. She accepted my gift graciously then squirreled it all away in her sack, her eyes darting from side to side.

"Everything around here has a price," she told me. "I can use these to trade for things like shampoo and soap."

"Next time I'll bring those things." I said as she motioned for me to sit.

"Don't worry about that now. I'm so happy that you came back," she said, tucking a wisp of hair under a neon orange stocking cap.

"I know it's none of my business,' I said, "but I've been wondering how you ended up here." I glanced around at all the guarded people, clinging to their meager possessions. A faraway look clouded Minnie's eyes. She stared out past the arched entrance where a streetlight glowed feebly.

"It was so long ago," she said, "another lifetime. I was married. We didn't have much, but we were happy. Jim and I had a baby girl. We named her Anna, after my mother. Things were good until baby Anna got sick.

Jim worked hard at whatever jobs he could find; construction, landscaping, loading trucks. We didn't have insurance. Nobody did. I found out later that if we'd taken Anna to the hospital sooner, she would have survived. She died of pneumonia. My sweet little Anna was only three months old."

A hiccup of grief escaped as my chin quivered and I fought back tears.

"Don't cry," Minnie said and placed her spindly hand over mine. "I've cried enough tears for my little Anna to last a lifetime, but it still hurts." She sat quietly for a few moments while she collected her thoughts. "Jim couldn't deal with losing Anna. She had brought so much joy into our lives. He started drinking heavily. He said he felt like a failure as a father. He went off to work one day—and never came back. I didn't have a job or any skills and ended up on the street when I couldn't pay the rent. I did what I could to survive, things I'm not proud of."

"What about your family? I asked. "Wasn't there someone to help you get back on your feet?"

Suddenly, something behind me caught Minnie's attention. "Mia, run!" she shouted.

Someone grabbed me from behind and covered my mouth. I heard a man's voice, "Get her gun." Then everything went dark.

~

"Where the hell is she?" Emma looked at her watch and then at Natalie. "It's getting late. I've got stuff to do. Don't just stand here. Go look for her."

Natalie took her Ruger from her backpack and stuffed it into her jacket pocket. She returned to the spot where she had last seen Mia with Minnie. There was no sign of them. Natalie asked a man sitting nearby if he'd seen where they went. "The girl ran like someone was chasing her." He turned and continued rummaging through his belongings.

Natalie clutched her gun and undid the safety, breathing in shallow gasps. The far end of the viaduct opened onto a park with broken playground equipment, the grass and bushes overgrown. She followed a crumbling walkway to a clump of bushes. There she spotted Mia's backpack with her silver keychain clipped to the zipper. She checked inside. Mia's Glock was gone.

Natalie ran back through the tunnel clutching the empty backpack. She handed it to Emma, stooping to catch her breath. "Mia's gone. I found this on the ground. Her Glock is missing. There's no sign of her."

~

When I came to my head ached. I felt dizzy and sick to my stomach. I was sitting against a wall in an abandoned storefront. A single bulb cast shadows on empty shelves and broken bottles. "Where am I? Where's Natalie and Emma?" I asked, rubbing the lump on my head. I was startled when someone replied.

"We won't hurt you," he said, his voice vaguely familiar. A ski mask covered his face but judging by his build and clothing I guessed that he was youngish, maybe Emma's age.

"Too late—you already did. What do you want? If it's money, I haven't got any." I was angry and aching and I surprised myself with my quick comeback. I felt around the floor for my backpack.

"Your cooperation."

"Where's my gun? Who are you?" I suddenly felt chilled in the clammy space. It smelled of mold and urine. I sensed movement in the back of the room. A slender figure approached haltingly. It took a few moments to realize who it was.

"You're in on this, too? I can't believe it! I trusted you. I came back because I wanted to help you." It was too much to take in. I wanted to cry, but I knew it wouldn't help my cause. I vowed to be strong.

"This isn't what it seems," Minnie whispered, sitting down next to me. "People on the street, like me, are easy prey, especially us women. I've seen it firsthand, Mia. Assault, robbery, rape, even murder. People just don't care. It's one less homeless person, one less vagrant. I've been attacked myself. We *need* protection," Minnie said with a glint of defiance in her eyes. "Juan looks out for us, gets us things we need but can't always get for ourselves like clothes that fit, medicine, toothpaste and brushes. Things you take for granted but we don't."

"I don't want anything to do with this. Give me my Glock and let me out of here! Emma and Natalie are waiting for me." I tried to stand but immediately felt dizzy.

"Helms knows. He's helping us," Juan said. "The girls in his club will do anything for him, including steal guns." I recognized his voice. It was Juan, the guy who greeted us on the field trip.

"What? I don't get it. He's unarmed." Nothing made sense. Everything I thought was true was a lie. I thought Mr. Helm's job was to teach us to be socially responsible, but he was just the opposite. I clutched my stomach to ward off a wave of nausea.

"Helms has a network of people working for him," Juan said. "You wouldn't believe how careless people are. They set their backpack down and in an instant it's gone along with their gun. Someone grabs it to resell it or pass it along to someone who needs it…someone like Minnie."

"Only I didn't set my gun down. You attacked me and stole it!" I rubbed my fingers over the throbbing lump on the back of my head.

"More than your gun, Mia, we need your help." Minnie scooted closer and folded her hand into mine. When I saw Juan coming toward you, I knew what he was going to do. That's why I told you to run. I would have tried to convince you myself, without hurting you. She glanced defiantly at Juan. At that moment, something shifted inside me, the one who always follows the rules, gets good grades and does what's expected of her. I knew that helping Minnie was dangerous and against the law, but suddenly I didn't care. It was the first time in my life that I was faced with being part of something dangerous. Mr. Helm and his followers were breaking the law to help the homeless and I wanted to be part of it.

"I've got to get back. Natalie and Emma are waiting. They've probably called the police by now."

"I'll take you back to the parking lot," Juan said. "If the police are there make up a story. Tell them you wandered away from the camp. I'll be in touch with you through Mr. Helm."

~

Juan drove me to the far entrance of the viaduct in a beat-up van, barely stopping long enough for me to slide open the door and jump out. Flashing lights were visible at the other end of the tunnel. As I walked under the arch Natalie came running toward me. "Oh my God! Are you alright? What happened?"

"Is this your missing friend?" A young police officer with close-cropped hair asked Emma as we approached.

Emma nodded. "Thank God you're alright." She said, hugging me. "I don't know what I would have told your parents."

"I'll need your statement for my report, Miss." He was not much older than Emma, probably new to the force.

"I slipped and hit my head. I must have passed out and when I came to, I got turned around. It took me a while to figure out where I was."

"I'm calling an ambulance," he said.

"No don't!" We responded in unison.

"Honestly, I don't need an ambulance. I just want to go home. Emma and Natalie can take me. I promise I'll be fine."

He looked at us for a few moments then said to Emma, "Okay, but keep an eye on her and get medical attention if she needs it."

"We absolutely will officer," Emma flashed her sweetest smile. She put her arm around me and led me toward the van.

"Jesus, that was close," Emma said once we were inside. "Is that what really happened or are you leaving stuff out? You were gone for over an hour. What were you doing, just wandering around?"

How was it that Emma could get inside my head so easily? Is it because she knows her sister so well and I'm just like her? Or is it because I'm a terrible liar? Maybe a little of both.

"Someone hit me over the head and took my gun. When I woke up, I was in an abandoned storefront and some guy was telling me that he needed my cooperation. It was Juan, the guy who came out to greet us on the field trip. He's working with Mr. Helm, stealing guns for the homeless."

"Holy crap," Natalie said. "I knew Helm was on the fringe, but not outside the law."

"That's not all," I said, wondering if I should tell them about Minnie's involvement. I wanted to protect her.

"What? For God's sake, Mia, I'm in no mood for thirty questions," Emma said as she sped up, shooting me nasty looks in the rearview mirror.

"Minnie's in on it, too. I know it sounds bad, but…"

"How bad is it?" Emma interrupted.

"It's dangerous on the street. Minnie needs protection for herself and other homeless women. She told me some stories…"

"So, you're with them?" Natalie wanted to know.

"I think so," I stammered.

"You're either with them or you're not," Natalie said with conviction.

"Then, yes, I'm with them. You'll help me, right? I can't do this alone."

We arrived at Natalie's house. Before we went inside, she whispered in my ear, "I'll help you, but don't breathe a word of this to anyone, especially my parents."

"Same here."

"Deal," we agreed and hurried up the steps.

~

From then on Natalie and I were on high alert for guns left in the cafeteria, auditorium, library even in a bathroom stall. When we found one, we discreetly put it in our backpack. If someone saw us, we took it to the office. Otherwise, we stashed it until we met with Mr. Helm at a park several blocks from school. Mr. Helm treated us like members of a secret club, not like lowly freshmen. Sometimes he shared his plans with us; "Don't come on the fifteenth, I'm meeting with Juan to unload what you've collected. You're doing a great job." He'd flash his dazzling smile. We gobbled up the attention like candy.

~

New Horizon was the boys' school paired with New Hope. It had the same rules and high expectations for its students. Although we didn't attend class with boys, we had many opportunities for after-school and week-end activities like co-ed volleyball, chess club, Spanish club and most importantly, dances. Natalie tried out to be a cheerleader for the boys' basketball team and made the squad. I didn't stand a chance and I knew it. I'd never even mastered a cartwheel. But I went to all the games and cheered like a maniac.

Teddy was a big deal on the basketball court. After attending a few games, it was obvious he was one of the top players. Plus, he was a *junior*. A very big deal. It was also obvious that Nats had a crush on him. She cheered especially loud when he scored and she hung around after the games to congratulate him when they won and console him with a pouty look when they lost.

Nats was changing before my eyes. She got her braces off and only had to wear a retainer at night. She began styling her unruly red hair into a French braid and she even started wearing make-up. When I asked her about it, she confided that the make-up belonged to Emma—mascara, eyeliner and foundation. I was more than a little jealous.

After a big semi-final victory for New Horizon, she came bounding over while I waited in the parking lot for Dad to pick us up. She was bouncing and squealing like she was on drugs, but her drug was Teddy.

"Guess what? Teddy asked us to go for burgers after the game! Can you believe it?"

"You go," I said, knowing that I'd feel out of place. I wasn't a cheerleader and what would I say to a bunch of jocks?

"But you have to," Natalie said. "I can't go unless you do. You *have* to do this for me."

She had a determined look on her face, her freckles were dark as raisins. When Natalie wants something, she doesn't give up, so I called Dad and said a bunch of us were going out for something to eat after the game and I'd get a ride home.

Natalie clued me in on Teddy. His parents were super rich and were constantly traveling, sometimes for business but mostly because they could. They trusted him alone when they were gone. He was on his own. Oh, and Teddy had a license—and a Jeep. How perfect was that?

The burger joint was packed with kids from the game and more continued to pour in. I noticed the envious glances directed at us from other New Hope girls. Nats and I were sitting with the winning team, and just as I'd feared, I felt totally out of place. I didn't know the music they listened to or the video games they played. They were a tight group that welcomed Natalie into their inner circle. I was invisible, sitting off to the side. I must have looked like a real loser. Eventually a guy I hadn't noticed at the games walked up to me and introduced himself.

"Hi, I'm Rick." He glanced toward Natalie. "She's really something, isn't she?"

Natalie was the center of attention with all the jocks swarming around her like worker bees to the queen, laughing and joking, having a great time.

"She's a force, for sure," I said. "I'm Mia, by the way."

"I'm Rick, Teddy's friend. We go way back." He told me that he had attended New Horizons a couple years before Teddy but was expelled and ended up at Jane Addams, the local public high school. I didn't ask him why he was expelled because, honestly, I didn't care. He looked way too old to be hanging with Teddy. He had what Dad called a 'five o'clock shadow.' He wore faded jeans, a flannel shirt and work boots. He looked like he could be a carpenter or electrician, but his fingernails were clean and his hands were smooth. When I asked him what he did, he said, "This and that, I do odd jobs."

Great. I'm sitting here with a stranger who does odd jobs. We ate our burgers and fries in silence. When we were done the server brought two checks which was okay with me since we weren't on a date and even if he had offered to pay, I wouldn't have let him. I didn't want to owe this guy anything. Finally, kids started to leave. Natalie came over and said Teddy would give us a ride home.

Natalie sat in the front seat with Teddy. Rick and I got in the backseat. I sat as far away from Rick as possible. Nats and Teddy were making plans for paintball on Saturday. She turned around, "You're both coming, of course." Rick grunted in agreement. I tried to think of some big plans I had for Saturday, but I couldn't come up with anything. Soon Teddy pulled up to my house.

"I need to talk to you—over here," I motioned to Natalie as we walked toward my front door. "I'm just saying, I'll play paintball with you tomorrow, only because I've never played and I want to see what it's like. But, just for the record, no more double dates. Rick gives me the creeps. I have a bad feeling about him."

"You're such a baby!" Natalie hissed. "You'll never have a boyfriend if you don't lower your standards."

"Oh sure, like you've lowered yours, dating the captain of the basketball team. You just want me around to make it convenient for you."

"Whatever," Natalie said, in a hurry to get back in the car and Teddy. She was ditching me for Teddy! My best friend was throwing me under the bus for a boy. I felt like something in my life was ending. I watched the Jeep peel down the street. I quietly went in the house, yelled "I' home," and went upstairs to my room.

~

I arrived at Natalie's the next day dressed in what I thought was paintball attire—an old pair of jeans and a sweatshirt. Boy, was I wrong. Natalie had transformed herself into a new-age princess; black leggings, a black camisole under a gauzy hot pink shirt topped off with streaks of pink in her hair. My first impulse was to laugh, but I didn't dare. I could tell by the way she pranced around the room looking at herself in the mirror that she thought she was hot stuff. And she was, but this wasn't the Natalie I knew—the girl I'd met only months before who smelled of peppermint. The girl whose emotions I could gauge by her freckles. Only now I couldn't read them because they were covered with make-up. I felt empty—and sad.

Teddy pulled up in his Jeep and Natalie shouted "Bye, I'm going" as she charged out the door before anyone could see how she was dressed. Were her parents okay with her new look? I wasn't, but I kept it to myself.

Natalie climbed into the front seat. Teddy exclaimed, "You look hot, Babe!"

Babe? Natalie was now *Babe?* I reluctantly got in the back seat opposite Rick. All I wanted was for this day to be over.

~

Teddy and Natalie were a team, as were Rick and me. We met up with more guys from school, but Natalie and I were the only girls. After we put on our matching vests and received our loaded rifles, it was pandemonium. Rick was a wild man, blasting everyone in sight with globs of lime green paint. I caught him aiming at me before I quickly yelled at him, "Hey, I'm on your team, remember?" I found a hiding place and stayed there, trying to avoid being hit any more than I already was. I was a walking mural of fluorescent pink, green, orange and yellow. After a few minutes Natalie came creeping around the corner, pristine as new fallen snow.

"How'd you manage that?" I asked. Her outfit looked the same as when she walked out of her house. Not a spot of paint anywhere.

"Teddy was protecting me, but Rick's out to destroy me. Can I hide here with you for a while? Teddy's off shooting the guys."

"Whatever," I said, trying to sound like I didn't care.

Just then Rick came around the corner, his rifle aimed directly at Natalie.

"There you are pretty lady. Looks like you lost your protector."

"Just go ahead and shoot me," Natalie said, sounding bored with the game.

"First I'm going to have some fun—you're my hostage, now."

Natalie cowered behind me but Rick shoved me aside and grabbed Natalie around the waist, dragging her away. My gut told me that playtime was over and this guy Rick was seriously unhinged. I ran to find Teddy and convince him that Natalie needed him, *now*!

"Okay, Dude, you win," Teddy said as he approached Rick and Natalie. "Let her go."

Rick stood his ground, one arm around Natalie and the other on his rifle aimed at Teddy.

"I mean it," Teddy said with conviction as he slowly walked toward them.

"Jeez, I was just kidding, can't you take a joke?" Rick said, releasing Natalie who ran into Teddy's arms.

That was the turning point for me. I knew then that there was something off about Rick. His feelings toward Natalie were more than just a crush. He was dangerous and there was no convincing me otherwise. Natalie tried making excuses for him; Teddy was Rick's only friend. His parents had disowned him. He didn't have anyone else. If Teddy stood by him, she would, too.

"Be careful, Natalie. There's something not right about that guy. I can feel it." She just laughed and kissed Teddy for 'rescuing' her. I could tell she wasn't taking my warning seriously.

I watched Natalie change before my eyes. We were still friends, but our relationship was hanging by a thread. She used me as her excuse when she stayed out past curfew. One night she asked if she could stay over after a drinking party. She walked in the door and tried to make it to the bathroom before barfing on the rug. Of course, I had to clean up the mess. When I brought the rug downstairs to wash, I told Mother that Natalie was caught off guard with her period. Why, I asked myself, was I continuing to cover for her?

Natalie was in her element with her new boyfriend and friends. I kept to myself and reminisced about the good times when Nats and I were best friends, just the two of us. We shared all our secrets, but now I was the last to hear that she and Teddy were going to the Spring Dance. I was happy for her. We still said 'hi' to each other in the hall and occasionally talked, but she was swept up with the popular crowd and didn't have time for me anymore. I was still collecting guns for Mr. Helm. I hoped that Natalie wouldn't rat me out to her new friends.

Weeks after the paintball fiasco, I got a call from Rick asking if I'd like to go on a double date with Teddy and Natalie. I'm not sure how he got my number, but I specifically told Natalie that I didn't want anything to do with him. I gave him a lame excuse, something about tutoring a classmate. He called me a stuck-up bitch and hung up. I blocked his number.

During spring break I thought about visiting Minnie, but I had no way to get there. Mr. Helm asked me why Natalie hadn't been at Social Action Club meetings recently. I told him the truth—that she was hanging with a different crowd. I missed her.

In class Mr. Helm taught us to question everything. Like how could more guns mean safer streets? Common sense said that more guns meant more potential for violence. It was a contradiction, he said. At Social Action Club he continued talking about the homeless and our responsibility to not only make life easier for them, but to come up with solutions.

Part of our routine at New Hope was unannounced armed intruder drills. We were so accustomed to flashing strobe lights and automatic locking of classroom doors from the inside that it caused little concern. We'd get out of our seats and line up along the wall next to the door so we couldn't be seen from outside the classroom. This morning's drill had girls laughing and talking, glad for a break from classwork. The announcement that followed sent a shock wave down my spine.

"This is not a drill. I repeat, this is not a drill. Shelter in place until further notice." A communal gasp was followed by sobbing and girls clutching their friends. I sat along the wall with the others. Minutes ticked by with no further information. What was happening? Was the intruder nearby? Was anyone injured? I couldn't just sit while an intruder roamed the hallways of New Hope. It felt like a violation of my safety and freedom. How dare someone break into my school!

Our math teacher, Ms. Fischer, removed the gun from the Plexiglass box. She seemed as shocked as the rest of us, pacing nervously while we waited for instructions over the intercom.

I needed to do *something*. I just couldn't wait for the worst to happen. It was Mr. Helm's constant harping about taking responsibility. On reflex I reached into my backpack for my Glock. It wasn't there. I'd never reported it missing after Juan took it at the homeless camp. Not even Nina and Dick knew that I was unarmed.

I looked for Natalie. She was sitting in the corner with her head on her knees. "Nats, Natalie?" I whispered her name. She looked up. I could see fear in her green eyes. "Give me your gun." I stood while she rummaged in her backpack and handed me her Ruger.

"What are you doing?" she demanded.

"I'm going out there," I replied.

"You're crazy. I won't let you." She stood up and tried to wrestle her gun back.

"I'm going," I said again, releasing the safety on the Ruger while I sprinted toward the door.

Ms. Fischer tried to block the door, but she had no choice. The only way she could stop me was to shoot me. The hallway was eerily deserted, but ablaze with disorienting strobe lights and deafening alarms. I stayed close to the lockers and made my way slowly down the hall, asking myself all the while where an intruder might enter the building. Where was the least secure entrance? I realized that the patio outside the cafeteria was unlocked during lunch hour. Students could eat their lunch outside or get a breath of fresh air. I cautiously made my way in the direction of the cafeteria. As I turned the corner I saw Mrs. Smith, my English teacher, sprawled on the floor in a pool of blood. Everyone liked Mrs. Smith because she gave us free time at the end of class to talk quietly. Her vacant eyes stared up toward the ceiling as if looking for answers. She was clutching a handgun.

I was about to feel for a pulse when I noticed movement at the end of the hall. A figure quickly disappeared around the corner. I continued walking, pointing the Ruger in front of me. I knew that if the intruder continued in the same direction he would reach a dead end. What used to be the home economics wing had been walled off and was now used for storage. He would have to double back and I'd be ready for him. I squeezed myself into an alcove with a drinking fountain and waited.

I stood plastered against the wall, my heart beating furiously. I heard footsteps. As they got louder, I stepped out from my hiding place. I gasped.

"What are you doing here? What do you want?" I demanded, adrenaline pumping through my veins. The intruder was Rick, Teddy's psycho friend. He had a wild look in his eyes.

"If it isn't little miss stuck up Mia, too good to date me. This is good—you can help me."

"Help you? No way. What do you want?" We were at a stand-off, our weapons aimed at each other. I was trying to talk him down, something they *didn't* reach us in Weapons Safety.

"I'm looking for *her*." He snarled. "Your friend, the other bitch. She thinks she's too good for me—I'll show her…"

Stunned, I heard Natalie's voice behind me. "Put the gun down, Rick. You don't stand a chance. There's two of us. Two against one!"

I didn't dare turn around. On high alert, every nerve ending tingling, I didn't realize that Natalie was stealthily trailing me. Rick slowly walked toward us, all the while aiming directly at me. I held my position, extending my arms, taking deadly aim.

"Don't do it Rick," I said. "I don't want to shoot you, but I will." We were at a standoff, both standing firm, neither moving a muscle. Suddenly, all hell broke loose. Rick bolted toward Natalie. Gunshots rang out. Natalie screamed.

"I'm hit. Damn it, I'm hit!" I turned, just as Natalie crumpled to her knees and fell forward.

Rick ran past me shouting, "I love you, Natalie. It didn't have to be this way." He was still brandishing his gun, pointing at the bloody figure lying face down on the floor. He looked up—directly at me—tears streaming down his face and aimed at me.

In a split second my training kicked in. I fired three shots. I threw my gun down and ran to Natalie. She was barely breathing. I turned her over as gently as I could and held her head on my lap, stroking her hair. Her face was pale, her breathing labored. I took off my blazer and held it over the gaping wound in Natalie's chest. Blood was everywhere. Between sobs I whispered, "I love you, Nats. You'll always be my best friend. Fight. Natalie. Fight to stay alive for me, for Teddy, for Emma, for your parents, for everyone who loves you."

I sat sobbing and stroking Natalie's hair, frozen in the moment. I felt detached from my body, like I was looking down at the scene from above.

"They're over here." A swarm of police and medics came racing down the hall.

I stood and watched, as if in a dream, as they slid a board under Natalie and lifted her onto a gurney. I began babbling about Natalie, me, Rick, and Teddy and how I knew Rick wasn't right in the head. Rick's body was placed on a gurney, too—with a sheet over his head.

As they wheeled Natalie down the hall, I called out her name and saw her eyelids flutter, open slightly, only to close again. My blazer, soaked with her blood, was still on her chest. The medics ripped it off and quickly replaced it with a large adhesive bandage that stopped the horrible sucking sound. I was holding Natalie's hand when they slid the gurney into the ambulance. I almost made it inside until a police officer kept me from entering the ambulance. I shouted that I was Natalie's best friend, and she needed me, but it was no use. No way was I getting in that ambulance. I watched as the paramedics frantically worked on her before they slammed the doors and sped away, sirens blaring.

An officer escorted me to a police car. As I got into the back seat I looked down and saw that I was covered with Natalie's blood, my hands, blouse, skirt and shoes. She kept repeating in a calm voice, "It's going to be alright. Hang in there." I was shivering, *how can it be alright? Nothing will ever be alright again.*

The officer in the front seat turned to ask, "Are you getting her statement?"

"She's in shock," she snapped, like she was on my side. I felt safe in the back seat of the squad car with her at my side.

~

The school was on lockdown while the police looked for another shooter. The parking lot was jammed with hysterical parents searching for their kids and hugging them fiercely when they found them. News vans with giant satellite dishes and antennas swarmed the school grounds, establishing a perimeter. Reporters held a mic in front of students and parents, hoping for a statement, as they fled, stunned, to their cars.

Mother arrived, pale and nervous, her hair unkempt. She was frantically searching for me when someone pointed to the squad car. She rapped on the window and scooted next to me hugging me and whispering, "Thank God you're alright." I sank into her embrace, thankful for this rare show of affection. I don't remember ever being hugged so forcefully by her.

Part II

2

I was in uncharted territory. I had never come face to face with a shooter, never had to fire my weapon to defend myself and my best friend, never killed anyone. Until today. My life was hacked into two distinct chapters, before The Shooting and after.

I mumbled one-word answers to Officer Ramirez's questions. Yes, I knew the intruder, yes, Natalie and I were friends, yes, he shot Natalie and yes, I shot him. It was a start but there was so much more to the story, like how Rick was obsessed with Natalie.

"I'm taking you home," Mother insisted, but I had other plans. I wanted to go straight to the hospital to be with Natalie. "Mia, is that a good idea? She needs her family now. I heard on the news that she's in critical condition."

"I need to go," I insisted. "I was there when she was shot and I need to be with her. Either you take me or I'll find someone else." Mother looked at me as if seeing me for the first time. I was no longer the little kid she could boss around, buying all my clothes and making every decision for me. My best friend was shot, critically injured, even dying. I was going to be with her no matter what.

Mother dropped me off at the emergency entrance. "You don't have to wait," I said. "I'll keep you posted. I'll get a ride home." Natalie was in intensive care, immediate family only.

I texted Emma. After what seemed like forever, she texted back saying she would come down and get me as soon as she could. I found an empty chair in the corner and waited, huddled into a ball, my knees to my chest, my arms wrapped around my legs. An image of New Hope appeared on the television screen; yellow crime scene tape stretched around the school. The running dialogue at the bottom of the screen reported that one person was critically wounded and one, the suspected intruder, was deceased. Names were withheld pending notification of family.

The longer I waited and worried about Natalie, the more terrified I became. I was determined to see her, to squeeze her hand and reassure her that everything was going to be all right. I desperately wanted to believe that this was all a mistake, that it wasn't Natalie lying in the ICU. That it was a horrible nightmare, and we would all wake up from this bad dream.

Finally, the elevator doors opened, and Emma stepped into the waiting room. Her red, puffy eyes and pinched face said it all. She clutched a wad of tissues.

"It's family only so let me do the talking." she instructed.

"How is she?"

"Not good. She's lost a lot of blood and the bullet shredded…" She stopped, struggling to keep it together. We hugged and Emma cried on my shoulder. She backed away and clutched my hand. "I don't want to cry up there. Natalie needs us to be strong." She took a deep breath, set her shoulders and pressed the button for the elevator.

Family could only visit once an hour for fifteen minutes. I waited while Natalie's mother went in, then her father. Emma gave me her precious time with her sister.

"Talk to her, Mia. The nurses said she can hear us even if she doesn't respond," Emma said before I was buzzed into the unit.

The ICU was an alien world, glaring brightness, flashing LED lights, beeping monitors, screens with real-time graphs. A nurse nodded permission for me to enter Natalie's cubicle. I wasn't prepared for what lay behind the curtain. It was Natalie, but it wasn't. It was someone who looked like Natalie. Her skin was eerily pale with none of Natalie's tell-tale freckles. Unlike my best friend Natalie, she was silent and motionless. There was a tube in her neck connected to a machine that huffed and puffed continuously beside her bed. Wires snaked out from under her green hospital gown and blood dripped from a plastic bag on a pole into a tube in her arm.

I sank into the chair, light-headed and sweaty. I began shaking and couldn't stop. *Talk to her, Mia,* Emma had said. I took Natalie's limp hand and squeezed it, warming it with my breath. I leaned in closer and whispered in her ear, "It's me—Mia. You've got to pull through, Natalie, you've got to. I don't know what I'd do without you. You're my best friend."

"Sorry, Miss, I've got to draw blood, you'll have to leave."

"I'm here for you, Natalie" I said, squeezing her hand again, "for as long as it takes." I took one last look at my friend, silent and defenseless, before turning to leave.

The next day I visited Natalie while her family grabbed a bite in the cafeteria. I played her favorite music on my phone, told her corny knock-knock jokes and finally, read a vampire saga from a magazine I'd found in the lobby, but she gave no sign that heard me or understood. My friend was slipping away from me, from all of us, and there was nothing we could do except pray. My parents didn't belong to a formal religion or attend church regularly, so I prayed to a higher power to let Natalie live. *Please, let my friend Natalie live,* I pleaded to a nameless, faceless being that I wasn't sure existed.

Day after day I visited Natalie, hoping for a miracle. I was on a first name-basis with some of the staff. I'd sit on her bed when there weren't any nurses around. I brought a tie-dyed bandana to keep her hair from spiraling in all directions, while I talked to her like old times before Teddy and Rick, when it was just the two of us. I waited and hoped for a flutter of her eyelids, a faint squeeze of her hand. But there was no movement besides the rise and fall of her chest thanks to the machine that breathed for her.

My routine became eat, sleep, shower and return to the hospital to be with Natalie. After a week the doctors told Natalie's parents that her brain was functioning in a primitive state. Emma said they could either have Natalie transferred to a nursing home where she would remain in a 'vegetative' state indefinitely or turn off the respirator that was keeping her alive.

On Friday afternoon, two weeks after the shooting, Natalie's Mom and Dad, Emma, me and some relatives I'd never met, gathered around Natalie's bed to say goodbye. Before the doctor turned off the respirator, a woman wearing a cleric's collar said a prayer. Then we all waited silently as Natalie made a few gurgling sounds and breathed her last. Natalie's mother was inconsolable. Her father put his arm around her mother, supporting her. I hugged Emma as tears streamed from our eyes. I kissed Natalie on the forehead, then walked out the door of the ICU and cried until I had no more tears. I was empty, a hollow shell. Life was pointless without Natalie.

When Mother came to pick me up all I could say was, "she's gone." She didn't press me for details. I went upstairs to my room, slammed the door and shouted to the heavens, ranting about how unfair it was. I threw pillows and books and whatever I could get my hands on. Poor Tinker disappeared under the bed, afraid to come out. Exhausted, I fell asleep and when I awoke it was dark and for a few seconds I forgot. Then the reality of Natalie's death came crashing down on me. I couldn't eat or sleep for days. I was a lost soul, wandering around the house like a zombie, breaking down when I heard a song that reminded me of Natalie.

Natalie's death taught me a hard lesson; don't trust the bastards that brain-washed us into thinking that we were safe because we were armed. We weren't safe. Gun boxes, safety training, armed students were all a cruel joke. Natalie had followed me into the hallway thinking that she was protecting me, that she was my backup. She couldn't have known that the shooter was Rick and that she was the target. The investigation later revealed that he had left a note saying that if he couldn't have Natalie, no one could. I'd known all along that Rick had a crush on Natalie, more like an obsession. I'd warned her, but she didn't take my warning seriously. She figured that she had Teddy to protect her. But what chance did anyone have against an armed psycho? It's kill or be killed. I've got Rick's blood on my hands, but I feel like I've got Natalie's, too. I couldn't save her.

~

Before we left to go to Natalie's wake, Mother handed me a pill. I stared at the pink tablet in the palm of my hand.

"Just take it, sweetheart. It will help you get through this."

I swallowed it dry. I don't remember Mother ever calling me sweetheart or any other pet name for that matter. I know she felt sorry for me, losing my best friend and sad for Natalie's family, but she didn't know how to comfort me. I wanted her to wrap her arms around me and reassure me that everything would be all right, even though we both knew it wouldn't. I felt like a walking corpse, bone tired and unable to concentrate on anything for more than a few minutes. My mind would wander back to the nightmare replaying in my head; me stalking the shooter in the hall, the fatal shots echoing off the walls and Natalie's life slipping away while I held her.

The parking lot of the funeral home was full. Police directed traffic. We had to park two blocks away. Dad almost had to drag me out of the car.

"I'm not going in there!" I protested. I couldn't bear to see my best friend lying in a box.

I began to cry and Dad choked up too, but quickly wiped his eyes and pulled himself together. Buoyed by Mother on one side and Dad on the other, they walked me through the double doors into the sickening stench of lilies. I'll never forget that smell from Grandma Dottie's wake. I've hated lilies ever since. They meant one thing to me—death. Every arrangement had them, like a requirement.

We waited in the long line that snaked from the casket to the back of the room and into the lobby, all the while inhaling the death stink. I wanted to punch the kids who were laughing and talking, making plans. *Show some respect*, I thought. *That's Natalie in there.* At least it was supposed to be. I'd know for sure when I got up there and saw for myself.

As we got closer to the front of the line I started sweating and shaking. I clutched Dad's arm, my mouth was dry, my knees weak. We were next in line. Emma was on autopilot, robotically hugging each visitor and thanking them for coming. She was dressed in black; blouse, skirt, tights and booties. Natalie's parents sat behind Emma, accepting condolences but barely speaking. They were zoned out, still in shock.

I stared into the coffin. Someone had played a cruel trick. Whomever was lying there had Natalie's lips and chin, ginger hair and lashes, but her freckles were gone, obliterated by pasty makeup.

"No. No. No." I screamed. I covered my eyes and turned away. Emma was at my side instantly, hugging me.

"I know, Mia. I know." Was all she said as she rocked me in her arms.

"I told Nats that Rick was trouble but she didn't take me seriously." I sobbed.

"It's not your fault, Mia. You did everything you could."

Mother and Dad tried to calm me and lead me away, but Emma and I refused to part. We knew Natalie better than anyone and we wouldn't be denied our grief. I'd never again smell Natalie's sweet peppermint breath or see her freckles darken when she was angry or excited.

Finally, Emma and I separated and the next mourners took our place. I don't know how Emma held it together. Her parents were frozen in their grief, unable to react. Everything fell on Emma's shoulders.

~

Dad was distant after the shooting, preoccupied with work, I supposed. I asked him to take me driving so I could get my license and the taste of freedom that came with a license. He gave me a blank stare like he didn't hear me. I asked him again. He brushed me off with, "Now's not a good time, Mia. Ask your mother." Ha, as if this was a good time for me? Mother took me for a driving lesson. She grabbed the dash so violently at each stop that I thought she'd leave a dent. This was never going to work.

~

My earliest memories of my father were of him working from home. His office was in a small room next to the front door, meant as a closet. As a family we'd eat dinner together and afterwards he and I would roughhouse on the floor. Sometimes I'd sneak into his office. He wouldn't notice me at first, concentrating on his work. When he finally saw me, he'd hoist me onto his lap and tickle me until I gasped for air. I didn't like the tickling, but I laughed and pretended I did because it was our special time together. Now he only came out of his office to grab a fresh cup of coffee or snack, shower or sleep. When I'd ask him what was up, he'd ramble on about cut-throat competitors whose only goal was making money no matter who got hurt. He'd started smoking again. I remember him making a big deal about quitting a few years ago, and now he was at it again. Mother told him he could only smoke in his office and when it was empty she'd bomb his room with air freshener. Something was going on, but he wouldn't talk about it.

Truthfully, I didn't know what my father did for a living. I knew he ran a business, but I had no idea what he sold, to whom or if he had business partners. Every kid wants to know what their father did and I was no exception. When I got up the nerve to ask, he always came up with his stock answer; we had a comfortable home, nice clothes, plenty of food to eat and cable TV, so I shouldn't worry about where the money came from. Lately, all he did was blow me off.

Now when I peeked into his office he'd say, "I'm busy," without even looking up from the screen, "can it wait till later?" Sadly, there never was a *later*. I just wished he would pay attention to me like before. Was it because I was too big to sit on his lap? I couldn't help that I wasn't a little kid anymore.

~

Twice a week Mother took me to a shrink, a thin woman with greying hair. Her wardrobe was drab and old-fashioned, but she had kind eyes and was pleased that I'd agreed to meet with her. Of course, I didn't have a choice. At our first session I said little, answering basic questions about school, and my friendship with Natalie. Even when I sat silently, she wasn't upset with me. She acted like she had all the time in the world. When I looked up from my hands in my lap she smiled with compassion, not pity. I didn't want anyone's pity. Mostly I wanted to be left alone.

As the weeks dragged on, I looked forward to our sessions. I hated to admit it, but they were a high point in my week. It meant peace and a break from Mother's harping that I get myself together and return to school. Plus, Mother let me drive so I got some time behind the wheel. She stopped grabbing the dash as my driving improved.

During the day I watched television in my pajamas or slept. I slept a lot. At my lowest point I hadn't showered in a week. Mother laid out clean underwear, jeans and a T-shirt, took my arm and practically dragged me into the bathroom and under a warm shower. I was like the Wicked Witch of the West, *I'm melting!* The shower felt good, I'll admit, but my heart was shredded and I wondered if I would ever be whole again. I knew I wasn't ready to return to school only to relive that horrible day with everyone staring and feeling sorry for me.

Mother spoke with Principal Newhouse weekly. She encouraged me to return to classes, ensuring that all safety measures were in place. But those safety measures weren't enough to save Natalie, or Rick, for that matter. He should have never gotten inside, but somehow he did. And they want me to go back there? No way!

~

As the weeks dragged on, I was bored out of my mind and agreed to giving school a try, but on my terms, like not wearing the school uniform. Some days I wore a black T-shirt with the words 'Never Forget' across the front and Natalie's photo on the back. Instead of the pleated skirt and saddle shoes I wore black work boots and jeans. I chewed my nails to the quick and covered the ragged edges with black nail polish and lined my eyes and stained my lips dark purple. Amazingly, no one challenged me. My grades plummeted. Before Natalie's death I had lost a few pounds but afterward I quickly gained it back from the antidepressants and lack of activity. Before I left the house in the morning Mother shook one of my pills out of the bottle and into my hand, watching as I swallowed it. Most of the time I only pretended to swallow and spit it out at the bus stop. There was a mound of disintegrating pink pills in a clump of weeds at the corner that got bigger as the weeks went by.

I was a rat on a wheel, going through the motions of living. I couldn't concentrate, didn't talk to or see anyone, considered suicide. It would be so easy to overdose; I knew where Mother stashed the pills. Part of me didn't want to die, but I felt like I was already dead, so what difference would it make? Mother and Dad fought all the time now, mostly about me. Things would be better for everyone if I weren't around.

It was only a matter of time before New Hope washed their hands of me. The principal called us in for a meeting. Sitting in the office with the sun streaming in through the window, I was shocked to see how grey and haggard Mother and Dad had become. They had aged ten years in these past few months. Ms. Newhouse explained that New Hope did not have the trained staff to deal with *my situation*. It wasn't fair to the other students that I didn't have to follow the dress code like everybody else. That, and I was failing miserably, even though I admit that every teacher gave me the opportunity to meet after school for help or do extra credit to bring my grades up. It seemed like such a monumental task, why bother? I just didn't have the energy. I wasn't the same person since the shooting. I was drowning, grasping for anything or anyone to keep me from going under.

~

At least Jane Addams High School didn't make me repeat freshman year. I entered as a sophomore. At my first lunch period Chloe and the same girls that bullied me in grade school approached me. Everyone seemed to know that I was kicked out of New Hope. I looked for an empty cafeteria table as far away from her and her group as possible, but they sought me out. Chloe jostled me, spilling juice on my chocolate chip cookie. My lunch became a soggy, inedible mess.

"Oh, sorry. Mia. That was so *stupid* of me! Welcome to Jane Addams and all the kids who didn't make the cut to New Hope. You look like you'll fit right in." she said, eyeing my black hoodie, heavy eye makeup and partially shaved head. The back of my head was cropped while my bangs hung past my eyebrows. Better to not see Chloe or anyone else for that matter.

I got all up in Chloe's face. "Leave me the fuck alone."

"Oh stop! You're scaring me."

Chloe and friends laughed as I dumped my lunch in the trash and headed out the door.

~

After Natalie's death, I stopped collecting guns for Mr. Helm. What a hypocrite he turned out to be! He was Unarmed and professed to be against guns, but he profited from recruiting students into harvesting guns for him through Juan and others like him. I didn't know who to trust or what to believe.

If Natalie hadn't grabbed another student's gun and come looking for me, she would have stayed in the classroom on lockdown—and still be alive today. I'm sure of it. She should never have followed me. She couldn't have known that the shooter was Rick and she was his prey. But, dammit, we shouldn't have been put in that position. We were led to believe that we could protect ourselves, but sadly, we couldn't.

Emma and I kept in touch. She told me that people said the most ridiculous and unhelpful things to her and her family at Natalie's wake and funeral. *Natalie's in a better place. No one can hurt her anymore. Things happen for a reason. Something good will come out of this tragedy.* The only insight I gained from Nat's death was that I swore I would have nothing to do with guns again—ever. Natalie's death was a tragedy that shouldn't have happened.

Meanwhile, Chloe and her girl-gang of identical blonde, thin, look-alikes were on a mission to make my life miserable. They were wasting their time, though, because my life was already a dung heap. And speaking of dung, someone, I can only assume it was Chloe, stuffed a bag of dog shit through the vents in my locker. That didn't endear me to anyone whose locker was within twenty feet of mine. My books and folders smelled like crap for weeks. Anyway, why pick on me? I was trying to disappear. I didn't enjoy being dragged into the spotlight. I wasn't a martyr for a cause. I just wanted to be left alone.

The cafeteria was fair game so whenever the weather was halfway decent, I took my Power Bar and bottle of water outside to sit at one of the empty picnic tables. My mission was dodging Chloe, but it was a game that gave me little satisfaction.

Occasionally, another student came outside for lunch on warm, sunny days. He was tall and muscular, with skin like polished mahogany. He was in my AP chemistry class, but like me, he rarely spoke. When he did speak, he had what sounded like an English accent, but not quite. I couldn't put my finger on it. His name was Debare.

It was a sunny November day, bright blue sky with high, puffy white clouds. You could almost sense the advent of cool days and frosty nights. We were the only two people outside, so I figured, *what the heck?* He looked up at me with liquid brown eyes as I approached.

"Do you mind if I sit down?" I asked.

"Please," he said, indicating that I should sit opposite him.

"You're in my AP Chemistry class," I said. Duh, of course, he knew that we were in the same class, but I didn't know what else to say.

"You're Mia, right? You're one of the smartest kids in class." He smiled and continued eating vegetables and rice from a reusable container.

I felt my cheeks warming, but I doubt he noticed under the pale makeup I was wearing. "You only sit outside when it's warm." I said, hoping to learn more about him.

"I don't like the cold. I'm not used to it. It makes me shiver." He smiled, revealing dazzling white teeth.

"I get tired of dodging the mean girls and having my lunch ruined."

"I see how they treat you. They are quite mean. But you seem to take it in stride." His voice was as smooth as honey. I loved listening to him.

"I don't know. It gives me something to do—fending them off. They're basically harmless. I'm hoping they'll get tired of picking on me and find someone else to harass."

"You are brave," he said with conviction.

"No one's ever called me brave before. I don't think I am, necessarily. I'm more of a survivor."

"You have sad eyes. Perhaps something happened?" he asked, his dark eyes scanning mine.

Just then the bell rang. I quickly stuffed my water bottle and wrappers in my backpack and left without saying a word.

"I'm sorry." He called after me. "I didn't mean to offend you." he called as I walked away. He had sad eyes, too. Sad, dark eyes. Was it because he had to leave his country or was he lonely like me?

~

Even though I wasn't collecting guns for the homeless anymore, I didn't stop thinking about Minnie. I hadn't been back to the homeless camp since Natalie's death. The thought of explaining to Minnie everything that had happened—Natalie's violent death and how I'd changed my mind about guns was too overwhelming. Since leaving New Hope and the stares of my former classmates, I began to feel like I had a purpose—to overturn the system that idolized guns.

The last time I'd seen Emma was at Natalie's funeral. We stayed connected by phone. Months had passed when we agreed to meet. We were each coping in our own way. Mine was to distance myself from people by wearing outrageous outfits and make-up. Kids and adults steered clear, and that was okay with me. I didn't know how Emma was coping.

"How's it going?" Emma asked while we devoured burgers and fries.

"Better since I got kicked out of New Hope. Everyone there stared at me like I was a pathetic freak. That got old fast, but it's no bed of roses at Jane Addams, either. I can't believe it's almost a year since the shooting."

"I know what you mean. When I transferred to junior college so I could help my parents, no one knew who I was. Kids eventually put two and two together and figured out that I'm Natalie's sister, but they didn't make a big deal of it. Mom and Dad are having a hard time, though. They can't accept the fact that Natalie's gone. Her room is a shrine. Everything is how she left it when she went to school that morning. The navy-blue T-shirt and grey leggings that she slept in are still on the floor, a half-full glass of water is on the night-stand. Strands of her red hair were all over the sink. I saved some and washed the rest down the drain."

Emma stared out the café window at the low, grey clouds for a few moments, "God, I miss her. If only I'd been there. I could have saved her."

"I was right there and *I* couldn't save her. I lay in bed at night thinking, what if I'd told the police about Rick's obsession with Natalie before he went ballistic. But until the shooting he hadn't done anything illegal, unless being mentally unhinged is against the law."

"She had a boyfriend, didn't she?" Emma asked.

"Teddy. They were quite the power couple, like, prom king and queen material."

"How did Teddy take Natalie's death. The shooter was his friend."

"Teddy was devastated, understandably. I heard his grades suffered, and he took time off from sports. But he bounced back. He's got his whole life ahead of him." I paused, "Unlike Natalie."

"My therapist says acceptance is the final stage of grief." Emma brushed a strand of hair off her forehead. "How about you? How are you coping?"

"I go to a shrink, too," I said, chuckling. "Mother insisted. It helped. She listened without judging or acting like I'd shatter into a million pieces if she mentioned Natalie's death. That's Mother and Dad's approach. Don't talk about it and it will go away."

After lunch I wasn't ready to say goodbye to the one person whose grief was as deep as mine. I asked Emma to drive me to the homeless camp to see Minnie. It had been months and I hoped Minnie would remember me.

The neighborhood around 1929 was the same. Fast food wrappers skittered across the street like tumbleweed. Graffiti scrawled across abandoned buildings. Broken glass glittered like fairy dust. Emma parked where she had last dropped Natalie and I off. It seemed like another lifetime.

"Come with me, okay? I'm kind of nervous. It's been a while."

"Sure, kiddo. Just so you know, I wasn't going to let you go alone. I lost my sister. I damn well won't lose you, too."

1929 was as depressing as ever. Nothing had changed. Folks slept on cardboard pallets under raggedy blankets, their belongings stashed in trash bags. The odor of unwashed bodies, rotting garbage, and human waste stung my nostrils. I began looking for Minnie and when I didn't find her at her spot I began asking around. Emma hung back and let me do the talking. Either nobody knew where she was or they weren't talking. There's an unspoken code among the homeless; don't give out information. Some folks were running from the law or complicated family situations and wanted to remain anonymous. Finally, a young woman spoke up. She looked normal except for the fact that she was crashing in a homeless camp. I could only guess what brought her here. Maybe she was escaping from an abusive relationship.

"You're looking for Minnie? She's not here. They took her away."

"What? Who took her away? Where? Was she sick?" I was stunned. Was she in trouble?

"A government type with glasses and sensible shoes—been snooping around for a while, asking questions. Minnie tried to ditch her, making herself scarce when she came around. Then Minnie dropped out of sight. No one saw her go, at least no one admitted to seeing anything. It's like she never existed, except for..."

"Except for what?" I interrupted, frantic to find out what happened to Minnie.

"Her stuff. She left everything. She must have left in a hurry."

"Where are her things, now?"

"I took them," the woman said. "I didn't know if or when she was coming back, so I kept them, just in case."

She led Emma and I to her space. A prime spot, she said, away from the wind and rain and dripping ceiling. She pulled a half-filled trash bag from under a filthy blanket and handed it to me. "Sorry," she said, "I borrowed her socks and blanket, but I'll give them back, I promise."

I knelt and spread the contents on the blanket. Emma looked on. Among Minnie's meager possessions were her hoodie, a men's T-shirt, some underwear, and energy bars. Beneath the clothes was a small book, the size of a paperback novel. The pages were frayed, some were loose. A piece of string held the tiny book together. I picked it up and ran my hand over the faded green cover. Was it a diary? It might contain a clue about where she went.

"Can I borrow this?" I asked, holding the book to my chest.

"I don't see why not. It's not worth anything to me."

"Thanks, I'll take good care of it…'till she comes back."

I put the book in my backpack. On the ride home Emma tuned to a classical music station, the result of a music appreciation class she was taking to boost her credits, she said. It put us in a thoughtful mood. Returning to 1929 dredged up memories of the past year and the last time we were here together. Two people I cared about were gone—first Natalie and now Minnie.

When Emma dropped me at home Dad was, as usual, in his office. Mother was hunkered down on the sofa watching a sitcom rerun. A cup of chamomile tea steeped on the coffee table.

"How was your lunch? How's Emma doing?"

"Emma's okay, but her parents are taking Natalie's death hard. They still haven't accepted it." I didn't tell her about our visit to the homeless camp.

"I can't imagine what they're going through. I should give them a call."

I waited for her to say more and when she didn't, I went up to my room and closed the door. I remembered what Emma said about Natalie's clothes and threw mine on the floor in solidarity. I propped pillows against the headboard and carefully lifted Minnie's fragile book from my backpack. Tinker jumped onto the bed next to me, nuzzling my hip with her pink nose. I thought the book was a diary, but it was a bunch of old receipts and notes wedged between the pages of a daily meditation journal. I flipped through the pages, not sure what I was searching for. A sheet of paper, creased and yellow, fell out onto the bedspread. I carefully unfolded it. It was a letter, written in halting cursive.

Dear Minnie,

I'm so sorry. I'm not strong like you. I can't stand to see you suffer. I'm going away. You deserve better than me. I love you, but if I was a better husband Anna would still be alive and you wouldn't be sad all the time. Forget about me.

Jim

I sighed and stared at the letter then gently refolded it and placed it back between the pages.

~

The next time I saw Debare he was sitting alone reading a book.

"What are you reading?" I asked, looking for a way to break the silence. We hadn't talked since I suddenly bolted.

"This?" He quickly closed the book and stashed it in his backpack.

"Don't worry about offending or shocking me, I'm okay with whatever. I try to keep an open mind." I said.

"What? It's nothing like that. It's about my country, Nigeria."

"Oh, I wondered where you're from. Your English is so…what's the word…proper?"

"That's because at one time we were a British colony. We're an independent country now," he said with pride.

"I wanted to tell you I'm sorry for bolting the other day. I *am* sad, sometimes. Honestly, I'm sad a lot of the time because I lost my best friend." I stared at my chipped black nails.

"I'm sorry. I didn't mean to upset you," he said softly.

"It wasn't your fault. You didn't know. It really sucks because I just found out another friend of mine is missing."

"Wow. That sucks."

"I know. It's a long story. Are we still friends?" I searched his eyes.

"Of course, always." He flashed that smile again, like he was glowing from within. I couldn't help smiling, too. At that moment I felt better than I had in a long time.

~

I thought long and hard about finding Minnie, but I didn't have a clue where or how to begin. I searched online for *how to find a missing person*. A long list of detective agencies popped up. I didn't have money to hire a detective, and even if I did, who would take a fifteen-year-old girl as a client? I couldn't ask my parents for help. I wasn't even supposed to go back to the homeless camp after the field trip with Mr. Helm.

I told Emma about wanting to find Minnie.

"I've got an idea." Emma said. "My mom works for SAD, the Senior Assistance Department. Appropriate, right? All the agencies share information. She might be able to help locate Minnie."

"It's worth a try," I said.

I didn't hear from Emma for a couple of weeks. Then she showed up at my house one day after dinner. Dad went to the door and called up to me. At the landing I saw Emma and Dad talking in hushed tones, standing so close that it made me uncomfortable and I didn't know why. Before Emma came upstairs, she said, "I'll be sure to tell my parents you asked about them," loud enough so I could hear. That was weird, I thought.

Emma tried to coax Tinker out from under my bed. "Tinker never comes out for anyone but me...and Natalie," I said and quickly changed the subject. "Did your mom find out anything about Minnie?"

"Yes and no. She can't find anyone named Minnie on the rolls for government subsidies, which is probably why she's homeless, but someone's been trying to track her down. There's been inquiries from Social Services. Mom says you should start there."

I had to put my plans to find Minnie on hold. Mid-term exams were coming up and I hadn't been keeping up with my schoolwork. I asked Debare if we could be 'study buddies.' We began meeting after school and I eventually invited him over to my house after Mother kept insisting that I bring my 'new friend' home.

~

I peeked out the front window waiting for Debare to be dropped off for our study date. My breath caught in my throat when Debare pulled into the driveway driving a dented maroon car. He not only had a license, but a car, too!

Dad was in his office and Mother was in the living room reading a magazine that gave tips on decluttering and creating a cozy, family-friendly home. Our house was neat and organized to a fault, but cozy and inviting—not! It was always Dad in his office, Mother in the living room and me upstairs in my room. We rarely ate dinner together like we used to. Mother prepared a meal, but if Dad or I were busy we ate when we felt like it. We seldom did anything together as a family. The last time was for Natalie's wake and funeral, an outing I'd rather forget.

I stuck my head into Dad's office and announced that Debare was here. Dad glanced up from his screen. Let's just say that Debare is so proper, polite, and clean-cut that I imagine he's every parent's dream. He wore khakis, a polo shirt with his soccer team's logo and Nikes. He shook Dad's hand. "Nice to meet you, Mr. Compton." I relaxed. I could tell he'd won Dad over by the way he gave Debare a once-over glance and smiled. I introduced him to Mother with similar results. The satisfied look on their faces seemed to say, *she's finally found a nice boy!*

Debare slipped his backpack off his muscular shoulders and sat down on my fuzzy pink rug. A few minutes later Tinker cautiously poked her nose out from under the bed and sniffed Debare. He reached out to pet her as I watched in amazement. Tinker didn't take well to strangers, hiding under the bed until they left. I couldn't wait to see what she'd do next. Satisfied with our new visitor, Tinker nestled in the space between Debare's legs and purred contentedly.

"Wow, I'm impressed. She really likes you."

"I like her, too," Debare said massaging behind Tink's ear while she closed her eyes and purred like a racecar. "We don't have any pets at my house. My parents are at work all day and say it wouldn't be fair to leave an animal alone."

We studied for the history exam, quizzing each other from our notes. Then he helped me with algebra. Finally, I closed my book and rubbed my eyes.

"That's it. My brain is mush. We need to take a break." I said.

I scooted up onto the bed and sat propped against the cushioned headboard.

"Come on up," I said, patting the spot next to me. We sat silently for a bit. Debare's hands were folded primly on his lap. I was fascinated by his skin, dark as chocolate and smooth as marble. I ran my hand along his bare arm feeling his warmth. My heart was pounding like I'd just run a mile in P.E. Debare's eyes were closed. I leaned in and ever so gently, like a dragonfly before it flits away, touched my lips to his.

"Your parents?" he whispered.

"It's okay," I reassured him. "Don't worry, they'd knock first."

What followed was my first real kiss. It was messy, involving tongue and saliva and a new and pleasant feeling *down there*. I sensed that we'd been at it for quite a while when Mother called up from the kitchen, "Are you two ready for a snack?"

I smoothed my wrinkled shirt and raked my fingers through my hair.

~

Our study dates became routine, studying for a while and then closing our books. We'd plop down on my bed, exhausted from brain exercises, make out and inevitably explore each other's warm, smooth bodies beneath our clothes. Things got intense, but Debare would always stop before we went too far. That was usually about the time that Mother would call us downstairs for a snack. After finals, which we both aced, we continued meeting in my room, only now we listened to music and occasionally watched a movie on my tablet before making out. One night when I leaned in for a kiss, Debare put his fingers to my lips.

"There's something I wanted to ask you for a while," he said with a concerned look, "Remember when I said you looked sad and you said it was a long story? No pressure, but do you want to talk about it?"

I thought for a moment, collecting my thoughts about that awful day.

"At New Hope Academy, before I transferred to Jane Addams, my best friend Natalie was dating a guy whose creepy friend, Rick, was obsessed with her. Everyone thought it was a crush, but it was more than that. It was an obsession. He tried to get to Natalie through me and I shut him down. Call it unrequited love or whatever. I knew there was something off about Rick and I warned Natalie but she didn't take me seriously. She blew it off.

Rick entered our school through an unlocked cafeteria door looking for Natalie. It was supposed to be a murder-suicide. Rick shot Natalie," I closed my eyes for a few seconds before saying the awful truth, "and I shot and killed Rick.

"That's why I had to leave New Hope. I couldn't deal with that memory day after day. My classmates treated me differently after Natalie was murdered. They avoided me like the plague, like being near me was bad luck and somehow contagious."

"I'm so sorry Mia. I'd heard about the shooting, of course, but I wanted to hear it from you...when you were ready. Thanks for trusting me."

My faith in God was sketchy, especially after Nat's death, but somehow the universe or God or whomever had sent this incredible person to me when I most needed someone to listen and not judge. He wrapped me in the warmth of his arms where I felt safe, safer than I'd ever felt, even as a child. With Mother and Dad love was conditional. If I did well in school and got good grades, made the 'right' friends in the 'right' crowd, I was rewarded with toys, clothes, and games, whatever I wanted. What I really wanted was to be loved for who I was—chubby, brainy Mia. With Debare, I didn't have to earn anything. I only had to be myself. We were asleep in each other's arms when Mother called up.

"It's getting late you two. Time for Debare to go." Was Mother so naïve that she didn't know what was going on upstairs, or was she too embarrassed to say anything?

It seemed that the closer Debare and I became, the further apart Mother and Dad drifted. While Dad had always spent a lot of time in his office, it now was his official residence. Did they even sleep together anymore? Hard to say since Dad spent half the night working. Mother read or watched television until after the evening news. Then I'd hear her trudge upstairs, slowly, methodically, as if her daily routine was a chore that brought her no joy.

One night I awoke with a headache and cramps. When I got up to get Tylenol from the bathroom I heard muffled voices downstairs. I stood at the railing and couldn't believe my eyes. A woman paused in the doorway of Dad's office. They passionately kissed before she tiptoed to the front door. She happened to look up. I gasped. It was Emma.

Of course, I couldn't sleep that night and for many nights afterward. I felt sorry for Mother, alone in the next room, unaware that her husband and my best friend's sister were screwing around. Was this why he was being so secretive, shutting me out?

Things only got worse. I was due for my annual weapon's inspection and I didn't have a gun to inspect. I hadn't told Nina and Dick that my Glock was stolen and I hadn't reported it missing. Since Nat's death I swore that I'd never have anything to do with guns and I kept my word. Now I had to face the consequences.

My previous experience at FIB, Firearm Inspection Bureau, was simple. I'd clean my gun the night before, make sure the safety was engaged, and show up for my appointment. This year would be more complicated. The inspector, a lady with spiky pink hair sat behind a government-issue metal desk and asked to see my weapon without looking up from her computer screen. I cleared my throat and rummaged in my backpack for the non-existent weapon. Finally, she looked up from the screen.

"Your gun, please, Miss...Compton."

"It's not here," I said, fiddling with the silver keychain with my initials.

"Well, where is it? She demanded.

"It was stolen." I admitted.

"Did you report the theft?" Now she was sitting up, glaring at me.

"I...no...I don't think I reported it. It was a bad time for me. There was a lot going on."

"Bad time or no, Section 5321 of the Firearms Registration Act requires reporting the theft of a weapon. Your parents can be liable if a crime is committed with it."

I stood there wishing I could cry at will. I conjured the image of Natalie lying in a pool of blood and the tears began to flow. I silently apologized to Natalie for using her death to get me out of this jam.

"Alright then, here's Form 3552, Lost or Stolen Weapon Report. Fill it out and return it online or by mail." I took the form and turned to leave. "You're the third one this week and it's only Wednesday. Next time take better care of your weapon and report loss or theft immediately."

Filling out the form and returning it via snail mail would buy me time. I wasn't sure how long the process would take, but eventually I'd be forced to tell my parents that my Glock was stolen and I'd never reported it. I'd risk the consequences. For now, though, I'd fill out the form and hope it took months to slog through government red tape.

Turns out it took a lot less time than I'd expected. Three weeks later Mother and Dad were waiting for me in the kitchen when I got home from school. Mother was wringing her hands and looked more pale than usual. Dad was waving the letter about the stolen Glock and fine for not reporting it. His jaw was set and his face had a menacing glow like he was about to explode.

"What's this about your Glock being stolen? Why didn't you tell us? This is serious, Mia. I can't believe you never said a word." He waved the letter in my face, proof of my guilt.

Mother took a softer approach. "It's okay, Mia. I only wish you'd told us. We'll buy you a new one, of course."

I glanced from Mother to Dad. It was time to tell them. Not the story of how the gun was stolen in the first place, just what they needed to know now.

"Mother, Dad," I paused, "after Natalie was murdered I decided that I would never carry a gun again. It didn't protect her, and it won't protect me, either. I was responsible for Rick's death and even though it was self-defense, I'd rather die than kill another person."

Silence hung in the air while Mother and Dad weighed my words. Suddenly, Dad slapped his hands hard on the countertop. I gasped while Mother and I both jumped.

"So, you're giving up? A walking target?" he roared.

"Don't you get it, Dad? Guns are not the answer, at least not for me."

Silence shrouded the room like toxic vapor. Dad realized that ranting wouldn't change my mind so he tried reasoning with me.

"What's come over you, Mia? Ever since you started going to Jane Addams High School you've changed. I had reservations about sending you to public school but we didn't have a choice. Now all you do is hang out in your room with Debare. We know what goes on up there. Your mother and I were young once, too."

"It's not Debare's fault, Dad. I decided this before I even met him. He's the only one keeping me from losing it altogether. Ever since Natalie...you and Mother...you don't understand. You're so wrapped up in your own lives that you barely know I'm here. You with your work, whatever it is you do, and Mother with her magazines. I'm suffocating here!"

"This isn't over, Mia. There will be consequences. We will be getting you another gun. And you need to cool it with Debare. Don't you have any *girl*friends?"

I resisted the urge to tell him that Emma *was* my girlfriend, but it looked like he'd taken her for his own. I didn't dare say a word in front of Mother. He stormed out of the kitchen and slammed his office door leaving Mother and I staring at each other.

"Your father," Mother began, but I didn't give her a chance to finish.

"Even if you buy me another gun, I won't carry it. I'm done. I did what I was trained to do and look how that turned out." I turned and slowly retreated upstairs, my feet dragging on the steps. I was tired of guns and school shootings and life in general.

I collapsed on the bed, drained. Tink hopped up and I tucked her furry body next to mine. Debare was the only one who understood me and he didn't even know what it was like to lose your best friend. The day Natalie died was the end of my world—Nats and me hanging out, doing homework together, mocking the kids who gave us grief for being smart. All gone. I called Debare. He didn't answer. I texted him. *Dick and Nina say to cool it* with a sad emoji.

The next few weeks dragged by like cold molasses. I zoned out at school, my grades took a hit, and I wandered around the house like a ghost. I saw Debare at school, but it wasn't the same as snuggling with him in my room. I was in a dark place—and my sixteenth birthday was weeks away. This was supposed to be every young girl's dream—sweet sixteen! Mother mentioned having a birthday party for me. *Poor Mother.* She meant well, I knew, but I was in no mood to party. How could I be since Natalie had been killed only weeks before my birthday. Any celebration of my being alive for 16 years made a mockery of Mia's death. I couldn't even think about celebrating. The thought made me physically ill; headache, stomachache, you name it. And besides, who would I invite? Debare and I were supposed to be 'cooling it' and I didn't have any girlfriends.

My birthday dawned warm and sunny, a perfect spring day with blue sky and puffy white clouds. I dreaded getting out of bed and dressed for school. I'd made it clear that I didn't want anything special to mark the day besides my favorite foods. Mother made pancakes with blueberries, a thoughtful gesture. She looked pleased as I scarfed them down before heading out the door. Since Natalie's death I'd lost weight without trying. Depression does that to you. I stopped taking the little pink pills.

At lunch, Debare sensed that something was wrong, but I denied it. I didn't tell him it was my birthday, choosing instead to revel in my one-woman pity party. The day dragged on. When I got home, Mother was busy preparing lasagna, a food I associated with happier times when we all ate dinner together. It was a time-consuming process; boiling the noodles, simmering the red sauce, frying the sausage, then layering all the ingredients in a casserole and baking it until the top was perfectly browned.

We ate dinner together that night. Dad opened a bottle of red wine and poured a sip in a water glass for me. After a sliver of coconut crème cake, with candles and singing, I retreated to my room, dreading and welcoming the solitude.

I texted Debare, attaching a photo of Tinker with the caption; 'I miss you' with a sad face emoji. Moments later I received a reply, 'What about Mia? Does she miss me?' I let my guard down and told him I missed him and that it was my birthday. The minutes ticked by. When he didn't reply I cried. Hard. Snot dripping from my nose, tears streaming down my cheeks. I was so absorbed in my drama that I didn't hear my phone pinging until I glanced at the message on the screen; 'Go to the window.'

Debare stood on the front lawn looking up at me, all preppy and adorable, motioning for me to come down. In an instant my sadness turned to joy. Grabbing my grey hoodie, I opened the window and climbed out, hanging precariously onto the sill. Debare told me to

"Let go. I'm right here." I landed in his arms, knocking him backward. We lay in the damp grass laughing and hugging.

"Come on," he said, helping me up. "Let's go!" We ran down the block to his car, hopped in and drove off into the night without any idea where we were going. Despite the evening chill we rolled the windows down, laughing, letting the wind blow all our troubles away. I never felt so free in my life, not even riding a roller coaster, sledding down an icy hill, or riding my bicycle really fast.

I stuck my head out the window and hollered, "Woohoo!"

"Hey crazy girl, its past curfew, your parents don't know where you are, and you're unarmed. If I get pulled over, I'm..."

"Screwed." We laughed hysterically. "Where should we go? What should we do?" I was intoxicated with the possibilities—and the increasing distance from my parents.

"Want to go to 1929?" I asked.

"1929? What's that? Should I know what you're talking about?" He turned to me with a puzzled look.

"It's the underpass where the homeless people live. It's where I met Minnie."

"You've lost me, Mia. Seriously, though, isn't that dangerous at night?"

"You're not chicken, are you?" I knew that was a cheap shot, but I really wanted him to see it.

"It's hard to say *no* to you." I studied his elegant features; broad nose, high cheekbones that any girl would die for, full lips that I ached to kiss at that very moment. I stroked his muscular forearm. His lips parted in an inviting smile.

We exited the freeway into the dismal neighborhood. Darkened streetlights hung like broken limbs from rusted poles, unlike the shiny new streetlamps that illuminated the streets in my neighborhood, a place where there was nothing to fear except boredom.

"Are you sure you want to do this?" he asked, as he pulled into the deserted parking lot, gravel crunching under the wheels.

"Come on," I said, "I just want to see Minnie. The last time I was here her friend said she mysteriously disappeared. I hope she's back by now."

It was quiet in the musty cavern. Most were sleeping, some lucky enough to have phones were drawn like moths to the glow of the screen. I stepped gingerly, shining my phone, looking for movement. Debare followed close behind. A dark figure approached. I lifted the beam and recognized Juan in his uniform of dark pants and hoodie pulled so tight that his face appeared mask-like in the opening.

"What are you doing here?" he hissed. Since I'd stopped stealing guns for him, he wasn't exactly thrilled to see me. I knew he was capable of violence. "Who's your friend?"

I pulled Debare close. "This is Debare. We don't want trouble. I'm trying to find Minnie. Do you know what happened to her?" Juan eyed us up and down.

"Why should I help you? I don't owe you anything. You decided it wasn't worth your time to help us." He motioned to the people scattered about his feet.

"Juan, I don't even carry anymore. I lost my best friend. She was murdered by a school shooter. Maybe you heard about it? Her name was Natalie. I'm done thinking I can protect myself or anyone else with a gun. That's a fantasy. A lie they told us so we could get up the nerve to venture out the door every morning. It didn't help Natalie and it won't help me or anyone else," I said, turning to leave. Finding Minnie seemed impossible now. The hopeless feeling seeped into my heart again. Minnie was just another face among the many transients who came and went without leaving a trace. It was simply about survival, eking out an existence during the day and making it through the night despite the crack of gunfire, drunken rages, even rape.

Life goes on for those who fly below the radar. Friendships are tenuous because folks move from the street to shelters then back to the street when their allotted shelter time is up. The mantra here was *'look out for yourself.'*

Before leaving, Debare and I walked the length of the viaduct and asked anyone who happened to be awake if they had any information about Minnie. No one knew anything about the waif-like woman with big eyes and hair like straw. They hadn't seen her in a while. Going back to 1929 was a dead end. There had to be another way to find Minnie. Contacting social services seemed like my next move. The last person with any connection to Minnie was the 'government type' who came snooping around asking questions before Minnie mysteriously disappeared.

Where was Minnie? Was she okay? Did she leave on her own or was she forced? Was she being held against her will? So many questions. Maybe the woman stalking her was trying to reunite Minnie with a relative, a sister, perhaps? Minnie never mentioned a sister. I knew very little about her past, only what she shared on the few occasions we were together. Minnie's only child, a daughter, died as an infant. What if she didn't die? I'd read about infants stolen from hospital nurseries. I tried to think of any reason why Minnie would suddenly disappear. Maybe she inherited a fortune from a long-lost relative. Stranger things have happened.

Disappointed, we left 1929 and drove to a popular make-out spot. I scootched close to Debare and rested my head against his shoulder. We sat like that for a while. Debare lifted my chin and kissed me tenderly. It turned out to be the best birthday ever—away from my parents and wrapped in Debare's arms. And to think I had been dreading this day.

~

Debare dropped me off well after midnight and hoisted me up to my window on his shoulders. I blew kisses and watched him drive off trailing exhaust fumes. Before getting into bed, I splashed water on my face and sloshed mouthwash, too tired to brush my teeth. My clothes lay scattered on the floor; I slipped a nightshirt over my head and lay in bed under the blanket wishing Debare was here snuggling next to me. An image of Minnie's face appeared as I drifted off to sleep.

~

Last night's dream was so disturbing that I couldn't shake it. It kept replaying in my head all day. I was walking down a narrow hallway lit with bright fluorescent lights. Photos of Minnie hung along the walls. The first was a photo of a beaming Minnie on her wedding day wearing a grey suit with a white carnation on her lapel. Her new husband wore a shirt and tie, his face clean-shaven, his hair slicked back. He had a hint of concern behind his bright eyes. Maybe he was worried about how he would support his new wife. The next photo showed Minnie in the hospital with their new baby girl. Jim was kissing baby Anna on her forehead. The hallway narrowed as I progressed, the lights grew dimmer. The final photo was a black and white image of Minnie the last time I saw her, brittle hair, hollow eyes. She seemed lost, searching for a way back.

Insistent knocking on my bedroom door brought me back to the present. It was Mother, telling me to get up so she could take me shopping for some *presentable* clothes. I hid under the covers and hoped she would go away, but, of course, she didn't. Eventually I perched at the side of the bed rubbing the sleep from my eyes before grudgingly getting up and facing this new challenge—clothes shopping with Mother.

She liked shopping at traditional department stores. I wanted to go to the trendy shops. She valued style over comfort—I was the opposite. It was impossible for us to find common ground. She took a black sleeveless sheath off the rack and held it up for my approval. "Where am I supposed to wear that—to a funeral?" I took a pile of clothes into the dressing room and came out wearing leggings and a crop top. Mother shook her head in disapproval. Then I slipped a pink tutu over the leggings. Same result. Mother ended up buying what *she* liked while I hung out at the cosmetics counter selecting dark lipstick and eyeliner that I knew she would hate. Lunch wasn't any better. I wanted spicy Latin food—she wanted a Cobb salad. We finally agreed on burgers at a local hangout. We sat eating our burgers and fries while the latest music blared. I looked up as Debare entered the restaurant and placed his order at the counter.

Uh oh, this is awkward. Debare noticed us and came over to our table.

"Hi Mia. Hi Mrs. Compton."

Before Mother had a chance to respond, I blurted, "Mother, do mind if Debare joins us? He can give me a ride home later."

If looks could kill, someone had better call 911. Mother trained her eye on me with newly sharpened daggers. "You need to be home by dinner time." Then she turned to Debare and smiled sweetly. "Sorry I didn't get a chance to say hello. It seems my daughter doesn't want me around. Have a nice lunch." She collected her purse and abruptly got up to leave. Debare and I exchanged knowing looks and kept our voices to a whisper until she was gone.

"Don't put me in the middle like that, Mia." Debare said. "I like your mother."

"That's because you don't know her. Her mission in life is to control everything I do. I hate it."

~

Where to begin my search for Minnie? I considered going to the Bureau of Records for Minnie's birth certificate, but I didn't know her last name or the year she was born so that was a dead end. The woman who came looking for Minnie in 1929 was the key to finding her. The homeless woman's description, government type with grey hair and sensible shoes, wasn't much to go on, but it was all I had. What was I supposed to do—pick her out of a lineup of Kennison social workers? *Think, Mia.*

On the next teacher institute day Debare and I drove downtown, pinging from one imposing government building to another. It was tough going. We were passed off from one agency to another, none of them helpful, maybe because my story was a bit lame. I said I was trying to find my grandmotherly neighbor who babysat me years ago. Each receptionist gave us a brief look, told us that without more information she couldn't help us and sent us on our way.

My story about the long-ago babysitter was a bust. Why would a couple of teenagers be looking for an old lady that neither were related to? It was a bit suspicious. Did they think we were trying to steal her monthly government check? As the afternoon dragged on, we decided to give it one more try with a new story—the truth. At Elder Assistance, the woman behind the counter glanced at us with tired, vacant eyes then checked her watch. Almost quitting time. I rambled on about my homeless friend Minnie and how she had suddenly disappeared after a social worker came to the camp looking for her. I was afraid she might be sick, injured, or worse, the victim of foul play. This agency was my last hope of finding her.

"There's only one social worker here now. Everyone else is in the field."

"Great!" I gushed, hoping my enthusiasm would spur her to action.

She pushed a button on an ancient phone. "Helen, there's a couple of young people here to see you."

We waited while precious minutes ticked away. Finally, a woman with greying hair and sensible shoes stood in the doorway behind the receptionist. This *had* to be the woman who came looking for Minnie, or maybe all social workers looked alike.

"Can I help you?" she asked, glancing at the clock on the wall.

"I'm trying to find my homeless friend Minnie who disappeared after someone who…after a social worker came looking for her."

She directed us into her office and plopped wearily onto her chair. "That's all we do here—work with seniors in need. Do you have any other information about her—birthdate, last name?"

"I first met Minnie on a class field trip bringing clothes to the homeless. I went back a couple of times with a friend. The last time I went to see Minnie she was gone. Someone there said a woman who looked like you was asking about her."

"That's not much to go on," she sighed, "not much at all."

"Without her last name and birthdate, it's almost impossible to locate your friend."

I fiddled with the zipper of my hoodie. "That's the problem. I don't know her last name or age. I only know that she was married and had a daughter who died of pneumonia as a baby."

I detected a glimmer of recognition—and hesitancy in the woman's eyes when I mentioned the infant.

"It's late," she said. "Let me see what I can find out. Come back in a couple of weeks."

That said, she stood up, our signal to leave. Not very promising, but it was a start.

~

Debare and I only pretended to 'cool it for a while.' I sneaked out with him whenever I could. My parents thought that I was upstairs listening to music, studying or watching television. I felt a twinge of guilt about lying to them, but I found it hard to believe that they thought Debare and I would stop seeing each other cold turkey. Didn't they remember what it was like to be young, to want to be with your boyfriend? We tried to be good, but things heated up quickly in the back seat of his car. It was always Debare who stopped, breathless, saying we shouldn't go any further, that it wasn't right. It wasn't, but I would have 'gone all the way' in a heartbeat if he was willing. Thankfully, one of us had common sense. I thought the guy made the first move when it came to sex.

Debare was my first real crush. More than a crush, it's what I imagined falling in love felt like, never wanting to be apart, thinking about him all the time. He was there for me, a friend and darn good kisser. I felt safe sheltered in his strong arms. I loved everything about him, the way he looked, the way he smelled, his muscular body, everything.

~

Final exams were looming and my grades were suffering from sneaking out at night instead of staying home and studying. I convinced Mother to let us study together again and she grudgingly agreed, but only if we kept the door open and sat on the floor or at my desk. It was laughable but it was a way to see Debare without bailing out my bedroom window. We'd sit on the floor propped up by cushions until our backs ached and we had to take a break. I'm a better note-taker than he is, but he's smarter than me overall and remembers important stuff that's not in my notes. Besides being the best boyfriend ever, he was a first-class study buddy. We were lucky to find each other and sadly, if it hadn't been for Natalie's death and my getting kicked out of New Hope, we never would have met.

When finals were over, which we again aced, I wanted to continue searching for Minnie. Her story drew me to her. She had suffered, losing her baby, her husband and her home. She was a survivor but beneath her shell I sensed that she was as fragile as a plucked flower left to wilt. I was drawn to her tenderness, maybe because my own mother was distant. I knew I should be kinder toward Mother, but wasn't it *her* job to show me that she loved me?

On a sunny spring morning Debare and I drove to Elder Assistance where we had last talked to the social worker. The receptionist remembered us when we asked to speak to Mrs. Rutherford.

"Oh, it's you two. I'm sorry, Mrs. Rutherford is not here," she said matter-of-factly.

"I know we don't have an appointment, but we can wait—or come back another time." I offered.

"I won't matter. She won't be here." She bluntly informed us.

Debare and I glanced at each other. "Oh, is she on vacation?" I asked.

"Mrs. Rutherford has left the agency. That's all I can tell you." She hesitated a few seconds before refocusing on her computer screen.

Stunned, Debare and I turned to leave. We had been under the impression that Helen was a permanent fixture, as old as the outdated furnishings. *She* had told us to come back. Now, suddenly, she was gone. Another unexpected disappearance made me more determined than ever to connect the dots and find Minnie. There had to be a connection between Minnie and Mrs. Rutherford's disappearance. Did my questions about Minnie scare her off? Was Mrs. Rutherford hiding a secret that was somehow connected to Minnie?

"What now?" Debare asked as we walked to his car. "It's a dead end. She was our only lead."

"I don't think so. Think about it—we were asking questions about Minnie and suddenly Mrs. R disappeared. There's got to be a connection. I need to find Minnie's birth certificate."

"But you don't know her last name or birthdate. It's like looking for a needle in a barnyard." Debare said.

"That's 'a needle in a haystack,'" I said, smiling, "but I appreciate the thought. For such a smart guy you give up too easily. Minnie is not a common name. Hopefully, the records are arranged in such a way that we can look up all the births to women named Minnie in a certain time frame. We also know her daughter's first name, and her husband's. This will be easier than we think."

"You are such an optimist. That's what I love about you." Debare blurted.

We stopped dead in our tracks and looked at each other. He'd said it—the 'L' word. It lingered in the air like a Valentine's balloon. We stared at each other briefly before I began giggling like a little kid. Debare smiled, too, and pulled me toward him.

"I do, you know." He whispered. We drove for a while in silence, a warm glow washing over us—until we pulled up in front of my house. Mother was peering out the front window like a bored housewife playing detective.

"Damn, I forgot to park down the street." Debare sighed.

"She's already seen us, we may as well come inside." So much for our happy bubble.

Mother was pretending to scrub the perfectly immaculate kitchen counter and acted surprised when we walked into the kitchen.

Hoping to avoid questions I'd rather not answer, like, 'Where were you, and what are you two up to?' I quickly asked, "What's for lunch?"

"I can make PBJ or mac and cheese. What have you been up to?"

~

The search for Minnie was harder than I had anticipated. Debare was right, it was like looking for a needle in a haystack. I became a regular at the Bureau of Vital Statistics. The plumpish librarian with the owlish glasses always greeted me with a smile. Luckily, I didn't need any special clearance to search their files. The problem was that even though I knew everyone's first names; mother, father and child, the system didn't merge all three. I sat for hours comparing all the 'Minnie' lists with the 'Anna' lists and finally the 'Jim' lists to find a match. It was exhausting, but I was committed. Sometimes Debre came along, but mostly it was me with my hidden bottle of vitamin water and energy bar (no food or drink, no exceptions). As I suspected, the shortest list was the Minnies. I deleted the ones that didn't fit into the time frame I gave for Minnie to give birth. I estimated Minnie to be around sixty, with a window from fifty to seventy-five. I never was good at guessing ages and with Minnie it was more difficult because she didn't use beauty products that women like Mother used to look younger. I estimated the age that she might have given birth to be between eighteen and twenty-five, but I didn't rule out entries beyond those margins. I didn't want to miss a possible lead by being too rigid.

This became my routine—take the bus to the Bureau or the library and try to sync the lists. It became my world, my obsession. Time with Debare was the only break that I allowed myself. Mother, of course, became suspicious, wondering where I went and what I did every day.

I patiently explained that I was getting a head start on next years' science project, using statistics and data to locate missing persons. It was brilliant, I thought, and not technically a lie. I'd become quite good at lying, not that I was proud of it. I rationalized that it was for a good cause.

My phone alarm was set for 8:00 am daily. While most kids my age were sleeping in or working summer jobs, I was pulling on jeans and a t-shirt, getting a quick cup of coffee and heading out the door. Finding Minnie was what got me up and out of bed. *Why the obsession?* I asked myself. Was it because I wished Mother was more like Minnie—vulnerable and affectionate? Maybe I was being too judgy. Mother was unhappy, but she seemed to wallow in it instead of trying to change her situation. If she'd only try something new: volunteer at the food pantry, join a book club, take up line dancing, anything to get out of the house.

But enough about Mother. I was doing the best I could to rebuild my life after Natalie's death. Maybe that's why I was obsessed with Minnie. Unlike Natalie, I could still save Minnie.

I'd been working for weeks and narrowed down the possibilities to fifty likely and another seventy-five potential matches. I was on a mission, but Debare was losing patience with me. He had soccer practice every day and some nights he was too tired to hang out. At least that's what he said. Was he losing interest in me?

"Hey, what's up?" I asked as we drove down my street.

"Not much. How about you?"

"I'm narrowing down the search for Minnie." Debare continued driving and didn't say anything.

"What's going on with us?" I asked, terrified that Debare might be seeing someone else. After all, most of my free time was spent searching for Minnie.

"You tell me. All I hear about is Minnie."

I was devastated. Our first fight.

"Is there someone else?" I whispered, dreading his reply.

"No, but…"

"But what? Tell me," I insisted.

"Not for me, but you seem to be obsessed with finding Minnie. Soccer practice and games take up most of my time."

"Maybe I am a little obsessed with finding Minnie, but I'm worried about her. I'm sorry if I've been unavailable." I couldn't imagine my life without Debare.

~

On my way home from the library on a rainy afternoon, I spotted a slightly damp package on the front porch and brought it inside. Mother was making tea and asked if I'd like a cup. I'm not a big tea drinker, but on this chilly damp day I accepted her offer.

"Who's the package for?" she asked as she handed me a mug of honey-laced tea. I hadn't looked at the label. I assumed it was something for the house or Dad's office.

"It's for me!"

I peeled layers of tape and bubble wrap uncovering a plain box. I opened it. Nestled in a bed of peanuts rested a Glock 42, just like the one Juan took from me at the homeless camp.

"Your father and I promised that we would replace the one that you lost. It took longer than expected. They had to run the serial number of your old one in case someone tried to sell it or use it for a crime. Go ahead, pick it up. Get the feel of it."

I picked it up, turned it over and quickly returned it to the box. Holding the cold metal threatened to unleash memories best left undisturbed.

"Mother, I told you how I feel about guns. I won't…"

"We're just obeying the law, Mia. We can't make you carry it, but we've fulfilled our duty under the law."

I wasn't in the mood for another pointless argument about guns. I turned to go upstairs to change out of my damp clothes.

"Don't leave it on the counter. Take it upstairs."

I grabbed the box and held it away from me as if it was contaminated with a deadly virus. I stomped up the stairs and shut my door, kicking the box under my bed. Tinker bolted out giving me an annoyed look. I'd disturbed her afternoon nap.

"Come here, girl." I scooped her into my lap and buried my fingers in her fur. "I love you, little Tink." I loved and missed Debare too. I snapped a selfie with Tinker sleeping on my lap and sent it to him with a text. *I miss you too. Sorry I've been such a selfish jerk lately. CU tonight?* I inserted a sad-faced emoji. I rummaged through my dresser for a dry sweatshirt awaiting Debare's reply. The soft fabric felt warm against my chilled arms. Still no word from Debare. Disappointed, I trudged downstairs to make a smoothie with almond milk, an overripe banana, some honey and cocoa powder.

"Where are you off to?" Mother asked after I finished my smoothie and headed for the door.

"Just to the drugstore. I'm out of that shampoo that I like."

"Dinner is in an hour. I'm making one of your favorites—bacon mac and cheese."

"Sounds good."

I set off for the local pharmacy where Natalie and I sometimes went after school to buy peppermint candy. I usually got a bag of chips. Nats was sweet and I was salty.

I searched the aisles looking for the personal protection section. There on display was an array of condoms. I was standing there looking clueless when a girl with lime green bangs sweeping over her eyes and shredded jeans strode confidently to the display and grabbed a package of condoms. Obviously, she was no stranger to the world of personal protection.

"Uh, excuse me," I whispered. She stared at me through her shaggy fringe. "It's just that, well, I need to buy some of *those*," I pointed to the condoms in her hand, "and I don't know what kind and if I'm even old enough."

"First time, huh?" She assessed my ponytail, sweatshirt with JAHS across the front, leggings and worn sneakers. "Get these," She quickly selected a brightly colored package and handed it to me. "They're pre-lubed, spermicide, ribbed, the whole deal."

I handed the package back to her. "Could you buy them for me? The lady behind the counter knows my mother." I handed her some folded bills. "I'll wait for you outside., Thanks a lot."

By eight o'clock that evening Debare hadn't texted back. I was having my own private pity party when I heard a soft knock on my window. I pushed the curtains aside to see Debare's head peaking above the sill. Laughing, I opened the window and helped him inside. My heart thumped in my ears, seeing him with his torn-at-the-neck sweatshirt, work-out shorts and new sneakers. Waving him over to the bed, I detected an unfamiliar citrusy scent.

"New cologne?"

"It's my dad's. A birthday present from my mom. Smells good, huh?"

"Better than good." I playfully nuzzled his neck, but he didn't nuzzle back.

"I was surprised when you texted me. I thought you wanted space to finish your project."

"It's been nine days and I did, I mean I do, want to find Minnie but I also realized that I miss you. Can't we do both?"

"It's hard with soccer practice and non-stop games right now. That and…" He stared across the room at a poster of a melting glacier.

"What? Are you breaking up with me?" I said, my voice quivering on the verge of tears.

"What? No. Of course not, but…"

"I don't want us to break up. What's wrong? Tell me!" I rested my head on his chest, lost in his warmth and the scent of his fathers af-ter shave. He lifted my chin. The softness of his lips always surprised me. From deep kisses to lying across my unmade bed to caressing each other's bodies, I knew that there was no turning back. Not now. Not this time.

"Wait!" I suddenly cried, sitting bolt upright. Debare looked puzzled at first—then disappointed.

"Hold on." I jumped out of bed and locked my bedroom door. This was no time for Mother to stick her head in to say goodnight. "I got these, just in case." I said, opening my nightstand drawer and handing the newly purchased condoms to Debare.

We quickly undressed and tossed our clothes on the floor. The sensation of our naked bodies rubbing against each other was an urgency unlike anything I had ever experienced. Debare hurriedly put on a condom. I thought I would die if he didn't enter me. I closed my eyes feeling every sensation. It hurt at first, then I got the rhythm of raising my hips to meet his. His thrusts intensified, he cried out and just like that it was over. He rolled off me, spent. I thought it would be like the movies where the camera scans the couple as they make love for a long time. We lay silently for a while. Debare squeezed my hand.

"Was it okay?" He asked, staring up at the dayglo stars glued to the ceiling.

"It was more than okay because it was my first time...and it was with you."

I sighed and drifted off snuggled next to Debare. When I awoke Debare was getting dressed. "It's late. I've got to get going. Are you okay?"

"I'm fine, but you wanted to tell me something earlier." I hadn't let him finish before I accused him of breaking up with me.

"Oh, that. My parents said we'll be making our yearly trip home—to Nigeria."

"Nigeria. That's so far away. Do you have to go?" I sat up, not ready for this news.

"I can't get out of it. My grandparents and other relatives look forward to it and make a big fuss about me. They think I'm a big deal here in America."

"But that's so unfair! I'll miss you."

Suddenly, out of nowhere, the unmistakable crack of gunfire jolted us to high alert. I bolted out of bed and grabbed my clothes off the floor. What was happening? It sounded very loud and close.

I ran down the stairs, pulling my sweatshirt over my head, followed by Debare. Dad's office door was open and the lights were on but he wasn't there. The front door was wide open. I looked outside. A car sped down the street. Lights blinked on in neighbor's houses. I heard sirens in the distance. I recognized the acrid odor of gunfire coming from the kitchen. At first glance everything seemed normal. I stepped around the kitchen island.

I screamed and collapsed to my knees. Mother lay in a pool of blood. Debare immediately called 911.

"Oh my God, oh my God, oh my God," I chanted, my body trembling. My first aid training kicked in. I felt for a carotid pulse. My heart was beating dangerously fast, but Mother's was not. I began CPR. My hands were quickly covered in her blood. With each thrust more life-sustaining fluid seeped from her chest. I continued compressions until the paramedics arrived and took over. I collapsed into Debare's arms.

"I've got a thready pulse," one of the paramedics announced. They worked efficiently, sliding a board under Mother and lifting her onto a gurney. She moaned faintly as they moved her. I followed them out to the ambulance holding Mother's clammy hand. A tall, thin officer stopped me before I could board the ambulance. This was the same horrendous nightmare rearing its ugly head. How could this be happening again?

"I need to ask you some questions," she said, gently guiding me to the squad car. I wasn't in any condition to resist. Debare sat next to me holding my hand.

This is my boyfriend. We were upstairs when we heard gunshots. It was about 10:30. My mother and father were both home at the time. No, I don't know where my father is. No, I didn't see anyone leaving the house. The front door was wide open like someone left in a hurry. My dad's office was empty. No, I don't know if my parents had any enemies. I don't know if anything is missing. I haven't looked. My mother is dying and you're asking me if anything is missing? I answered her questions robotically. The reality of what had happened hadn't sunk in yet.

Multiple squad cars and news trucks lined the street. Yellow crime scene tape encircled the house, the kind you see on television, only this was *my* street and *my* house.

This wasn't supposed to happen in my quiet neighborhood. Flashbacks of Natalie's death washed over me. *That* wasn't supposed to happen, either. What was going on? Had I done something to cause my best friend's death and now this? It was the ultimate violation. Someone entered my house, *my* house, and shot my mother. I had no idea who or why. Where was Dad? Did he run out the door to catch the shooter?

The police officer said the house was a sealed crime scene until the detectives finished collecting evidence. "Do you have somewhere to stay for the next few days?" she asked with motherly concern. Debare squeezed my hand.

"She can stay at my house, officer." Of course, I'd stay at his house. Where else would I go?

"Can I see my mother now?' I asked in a whispery voice that I didn't recognize as my own.

"Yes. But only family members." She glanced at Debare.

We walked slowly down the street to Debare's car. I felt like I was drowning, swept under a towering wave. Debare tried to reassure me that everything would be alright, but how could he know? How could anyone know?

Debate started the engine and began to pull away from the curb.

"Tinker! I can't leave her. Please, we've got to go back and get her. She'll come to you."

I convinced an officer to let him into the house. Minutes later Debare handed me a shivering Tinker. I buried my face in her fur and held her close until she calmed. Debare remembered to grab Tink's food and her bowls. With Tinker safe, all I wanted to do was get to the hospital to see Mother.

I marched up to the reception desk. "My mother's here! I need to see her!" The woman behind the glass, numbed by constant exposure to human tragedy, took my name and calmly instructed me to have a seat. Someone would be out to talk to me as soon as possible. I reluctantly turned and sat while Debare parked the car.

"How is she?" Breathless, Debare rushed to my side.

"I don't know. No one has told me anything except to wait here." I clutched his hand, it was warm, just like his body when we made love. It seemed like ages ago. Another lifetime.

"Are you Mia Compton?"

I looked up at the woman standing before me. *It's her!* My brain screamed.

"I'm Helen from social services. Your mother is in surgery. They're doing everything they can for her." She glanced from me to Debare. There wasn't a glimmer of recognition in her eyes. "It may be a long wait. I'll keep you posted on her condition."

When she left Debare and I looked at each other. "It's her. It's definitely her." I said. Debare agreed. There was no doubt that this was the same woman that suddenly left the senior services agency. She didn't give the slightest indication that she recognized us. But there were more important things to worry about, like how was Mother and would she survive?

Waiting was excruciating. It was after midnight. I slumped next to Debare and dozed on and off. Each time I drifted off a terrifying darkness engulfed me. Then I awoke to the real nightmare.

Finally, the social worker reappeared and escorted me past the Authorized Personnel Only sign into a small office. I sat down on a worn upholstered chair and waited...again. A tall surgeon with wisps of greying hair sticking out from under his paper cap entered the room.

He sighed as he leaned against the desk and looked at me with tired eyes.

"We did everything we could to save your mother but the damage from the gunshots was too great. We worked on her a long time. Her heart stopped twice on the table and the third time we couldn't revive her." He hesitated respectfully then said, "I'm very sorry for your loss."

Part III

3

I was numb, like I had been drugged and couldn't move my arms or legs. I gasped for breath, certain I was having a heart attack.

"Take a deep breath and let it out slowly," the social worker said with authority. "You're having a panic attack."

Of course, I was. Violence had violated my life, again, this time taking my mother. I wanted to disappear, pull the covers over my head and never wake up. I didn't cry. I couldn't process the fact that Mother didn't make it.

Debare called home and arranged it so I could crash in the guest bedroom at his house. When we got there I leaned into Debare as he helped me upstairs. His mother had thoughtfully set a blanket on the floor for Tinker. Even in my grief-stricken stupor, I noticed that Mrs. Adebayo was tall and athletic, like her son, with finely chiseled features, also like him. I crawled into the bed and pulled the covers up to my eyes. The last thing I remember was Debare sitting next to me, holding my hand, his profile backlit by the nightstand lamp.

The next morning, I wandered downstairs to the aroma of bacon. Debare was sitting at the kitchen island with his earbuds plugged in. He quickly plucked them out when he saw me.

"My parents are at work. Mom said to make you whatever you want. I started with bacon."

"You can cook?" I tried to decide if I was hungry. "Can you make French toast?"

"My specialty. Coming right up."

He placed a plate of French toast in front of me, complete with a dusting of powdered sugar and maple syrup.

"Just like my mother's," I said before the realization of what happened came crashing down. I had temporarily blocked the image of Mother lying on the kitchen floor, her lifeblood seeping out. I took a bite of the French toast and crispy bacon and pushed the plate aside. We sat in silence for a while.

"What am I going to do, Debare? My mother is gone. I don't know where my dad is or if he's even alive. I don't have any close relatives. I have an aunt, my mother's sister, who lives somewhere on the West Coast, but I don't know how to contact her. My father has a brother but we haven't seen or heard from him in years. What am I going to do? I can't ever go back to that house." I felt the tears welling up. Debare knew me well enough not to say, *don't cry, everything will be okay.* Because clearly everything was not going to be okay today or ever again. He put his arm on my shoulder and pulled me close while I cried and sobbed and howled at the injustice of it all.

After I calmed down, Debare reassured me that I could stay for as long as I wanted.

"My dad's a lawyer with a lot of connections. He'll figure something out. We'll talk to him tonight."

Turns out Debare was right about his dad having connections through his firm. I told him everything I knew about my parents—where they grew up, my mother's maiden name, where they went to college. He said he'd take care of it. Within a week he'd contacted my father's brother, my Uncle John. He lived alone, didn't have kids—and wasn't interested in raising his estranged brother's teenage daughter. I was relieved that I didn't have to leave Kennison and move in with some old guy who didn't like kids. Ugh!

Next, he tracked down Aunt Joan, my mother's sister. She lived in a small community of ageing hippies in northern California and had a record of drug arrests. She asked if I was 'high maintenance' and agreed to meet with me if someone paid for her airfare to Kennison. Debare's dad was skeptical and I wasn't thrilled about moving to a backwater town with a zoned out ex-hippie. No wonder my parents never talked about their siblings. Debare's father asked if my parents had a will. I didn't have a clue and wouldn't know where to begin to look. Days after the shooting, there was still no word of my father. I needed him. Where was he? Was he even alive?

~

The week following Mother's death was a blur. I slept most of the day and didn't answer my phone unless it was Debare. While his parents were at work he was either at the gym or soccer practice. He gave me a single rose from a convenience store and I cried for a half hour. We tried playing board games to pass the time, but I couldn't concentrate long enough to finish a game of Scrabble. Monopoly was out of the question. The most I could manage was Sorry. We laughed sending each other's pieces back to Start. After a couple of games I was exhausted and needed a nap.

One afternoon Debare and I sat at the kitchen counter eating chips and salsa. I had blocked the phone numbers of reporters who wanted to interview me. I recognized the number of an incoming call, though, and answered it immediately. It was Emma.

"Mia? It that you? I've been calling and calling. I'm so sorry, Mia. It's unbelievable. First Natalie, now this. Unreal. Mia? Are you there?"

"I'm here."

"My parents heard sirens in the neighborhood. They have a friend on the force and called him to find out what was going on. The neighborhood is usually so quiet. I'm so sorry, Mia." There was another awkward pause. "You know I moved out of my parents' house, right?"

I didn't.

"I have an apartment in Anders, about twenty minutes from Kennison. I helped my parents through the worst of their grief after losing Natalie. I was grieving too, but I had school to keep me busy. The longer I stayed, the more dependent on me they became. I was doing things for them that they could do for themselves, like grocery shopping and driving them to the doctor. It was unhealthy for everyone. It was time for me to move on."

"It's probably for the best," I said flatly, although I couldn't say what was best for anyone.

"I want to see you. I'm coming over so we can talk." Emma said.

I explained that I wasn't staying at the house. I wouldn't stay there alone. I gave her directions to Debare's house.

"Who's Debare?"

"He's my boyfriend from Jane Addams. He's my lifeline, really. We were upstairs when it happened."

"And your dad? What about him? I heard that he's been missing since the shooting."

"No one knows where he is. The last time I saw him he was in his office. Debare and I heard gunfire and ran downstairs. The front door was wide open and he was gone."

When Emma walked in the door I could see that she had changed; her hair was in a stylish bob, she wore a blouse and slacks and carried a purse instead of a backpack. I invited her inside. She took a few moments to look around.

"This is some house. It's huge. What did you say Debare's parents did for a living?"

"His dad is a lawyer and his mother teaches at the university. Come on upstairs. I'll show you my room—well, the room where I'm staying."

"Sounds permanent, like you've moved in for good."

"I'm lucky to be here. I had nowhere to go. My weird relatives don't want me—and honestly, the feeling is mutual."

Emma and I talked non-stop for the next two hours. She told me about her tiny apartment furnished with thrift-store furniture. "It's small, but it's home, for now, anyway."

Emma became my second life-support, after Debare. Although nobody could ever take Natalie's place, Emma became a close second. The nagging doubts about Emma and my father were still there, but I needed her. My support system had dwindled to her and Debare, and I couldn't risk losing either of them.

One day I caught her off guard and blurted, "Do you know where my father is?"

She hesitated and replied, "No, why would I?" I didn't press her, the image of them together outside his office lingered.

Emma prepared me for returning to school, like how to answer insensitive questions like the ones she'd had to deal with after Natalie's death. And, of course, Debare would be there to run interference if I needed him. He'd already heard a nasty rumor from his team-mates that my father had murdered my mother and was on the run. He gave me a heads-up so I could call out the gossip mongers before things got out of hand.

I refused to accept the possibility that Dad had anything to do with Mother's death. Their marriage wasn't the greatest, but they never seemed angry with each other for long. It was me they were angry with for not carrying a gun. Maybe Dad ran out of the house to catch the killers, or maybe he was kidnapped. I couldn't prove either theory. It seemed a long shot but maybe Mother's death had something to do with his business. Maybe he was the real target and Mother was collateral damage.

A few days after I was back at school some guys cornered me by my locker. *This is what Debare had warned me about.* One guy got all up in my face, "So why'd he do it—your dad?" I could see the peach fuzz on his pimply chin. I didn't know him, but he seemed to be the leader of the motley group, neither jocks nor brainiacs.

"Excuse me? Get out of my face and leave me alone." I tried to squeeze past them but they blocked my escape.

"You know what I'm talking about. Your dad offed your mom and skipped town."

"Leave me the fuck alone!" I fought back tears as I plowed past them and ran to the girls' bathroom. Debare had warned me, but it still hurt. I was a ticking time-bomb. My rage was bubbling up, but I had no outlet for it. If Chloe or one of her hangers-on came through the door this minute, I'd punch her in the face for the hell of it. It wouldn't change anything, but I might feel better.

Chloe walks into the bathroom. I pounce and pummel her, splitting her lip and drawing blood until she begs me to stop, crying and asking what she did wrong. To which I reply, all the while slapping and punching her, "What did you do? What did you do? I'll tell you what you did!

Imagining the attack helped blow off steam. Chloe was only a scapegoat, though. I was angry about so many things. There were the mean boys, Natalie, for leaving me, Mother, for dying before we ever got to know one another, and Dad for disappearing when I needed him most.

~

I had forgotten about Debare's upcoming trip to Nigeria, the two-months long trip that included visiting his extended family scattered throughout the Nigerian countryside. Could I please come along, I pleaded with Debare's father. He said it was impossible. I didn't have a passport and I was a witness in an unsolved murder investigation. I overheard Debare's parents talking about 'foster care' one evening after dinner. My temporary stay with Debare and his family would soon end and I had nowhere to go. My future was looking bleak—homeless and without Debare.

"You will stay with me, no questions asked," Emma insisted when I explained the situation over lunch at our favorite burger place. She was the logical choice, she said. She was my only choice. "I'm working and going to school now, so I won't be around much, but you'll have the place to yourself when I'm gone."

"Can Tinker come, too?" I asked. I couldn't possibly leave her behind after all we'd been though.

"Of course," Emma said with a toothy smile that momentarily reminded me of Natalie. "I've always wanted a pet."

There were hints in her apartment of an ex-boyfriend, perhaps, that Emma hadn't mentioned; a comb in the sofa cushions, a single white athletic sock under the bed, a disposable razor in the shower, the same brand my father used. Emma said she would sleep on the sofa, but I wouldn't hear of it. She was dividing her time between school and work and needed her sleep. We shared the full-size bed. I welcomed her warmth next to me. She did steal the covers, though, and I yanked them back.

Emma's apartment was outside the school district boundaries, so there was no bus service. Emma drove me but I had to get up early. She'd make a pot of coffee and lure me from under the covers with a mug of sweet, milky coffee to jump start my day.

Not surprisingly, I had trouble sleeping. For weeks I walked around like a zombie until I read that having a routine and regular bedtime helped. Mine became homework, TV (unfortunately, Emma couldn't afford cable), a snack, then collapse into bed. One night I dreamed I was running down a dark hallway calling for my dad while someone chased me. Emma nudged me, "Sweetie, you're having a nightmare." My pajamas were soaked with sweat. Some nights I lay in a dreamless coma.

One evening, just as I was falling asleep, I heard Emma talking to someone. At first, I thought she was on the phone. She shushed whomever she was talking to.

"She'll hear us. You shouldn't be here. It's too dangerous."

My feet hit the floor just as Emma was closing the door. I bolted past her in time to see a man walking quickly down the hall toward the elevator.

"Hey wait!" I called.

The man turned. He was wearing baggy jeans, a flannel shirt over a faded green T-shirt, work boots and a ball cap. My jaw dropped. It was my father, who always dressed in pressed khakis and a dress shirt open at the neck. I would not have recognized him in passing, but that was the point. We paused, took a few steps toward each other and stopped.

"Dad? What?" I was torn between shock at seeing him, happiness that he was alive, and anger that he hadn't reached out to me. I had so many questions I couldn't begin to form them into sentences. He moved closer and hugged me. At first my arms hung limply at my side, then I hugged him back. He stepped back, looked me in the eye, his hands planted on my shoulders.

"I came to make sure you're alright. I haven't abandoned you. I've been following your every move, making sure you're safe."

The initial shock gave way to anger. *He was hiding from the authorities because he had something to do with Mother's death!* "Really, Dad? Because I don't feel safe. I thought you were either dead or kidnapped and that I'm the next target."

Suddenly the elevator dinged. As the passengers exited Dad shoved a roll of bills in my hand and bounded down the fire exit stairs. I stood in the hallway, speechless. Emma waved me back into the apartment and closed the door. I sank into the lumpy sofa. I didn't know what to think. On the one hand Dad was alive. I wasn't an orphan as I had feared. On the other hand, things were more complicated, not less. Was my father responsible for Mother's death? Replaying our meeting in my mind, he didn't mention Mother at all.

"Emma, tell me the truth. What's going on? Obviously, you two have been in touch all along. What's the connection?" My muscles tensed and I felt a headache brewing.

"When it's safe I'll tell you everything, but not now. The less you know the better." She was pacing the few steps between the tiny kitchen and the sagging sofa.

"Am I just supposed to accept that—after seeing my mother murdered and my father disappear only to reappear at *your* apartment? What are you hiding?" Now we were standing toe to toe, Emma taller and stronger, glaring down at me. I slapped her—hard. I had no place to turn, no one to trust. Emma betrayed me and Debare was a world away. Emma put her hand to her cheek and stood her ground.

"I want to tell you but I can't. I promised your dad." She frowned, caught between her promise to him and her friendship with me. But was she really my friend or had she been setting me up all along? What was she—what were they hiding? The image of them kissing outside Dad's office after Mother had gone to bed resurfaced. I had tried to forget, but it came rushing back.

"Are you sleeping with him? Please tell me you're not!" I shouted, but she just stood there, her silence telling me all I needed to know. I slammed into the bedroom and sank onto the bed, shaking with anger and sobbing with frustration. The reality of my situation slowly sunk in; my father and my best friend's sister were together and involved in my mother's death. My life was crap. Debare was thousands of miles away, without cell service, and not coming back any time soon. I had no one to turn to, no one I could trust.

I awoke the next morning to an empty apartment, half a pot of coffee and an overpowering urge to visit the homeless camp with the outside hope that Minnie had returned. I'd tell her everything that happened and maybe she'd have an idea. I called for an Uber and in a few minutes a car was outside waiting for me.

I tried to explain to the driver that I wanted to go to the homeless camp under the 1929 viaduct in Kennison, but she had no clue what I was talking about. After a few minutes of online searching, we were on our way. The surroundings were the same; litter, weedy gravel parking lot, boarded up store fronts.

"If I don't return in twenty minutes, call the police."

"This place is creepy. It's gonna cost extra. I can't promise I'll still be here if I feel threatened."

I walked briskly toward the viaduct, a girl on a mission to find my homeless friend. I continued walking through the dim tunnel, stepping gingerly.

Backlit by sunlight at the opposite end of the tunnel stood a familiar figure.

"I knew you'd come back. This place gets in your head." It was Juan in his usual black outfit. "She's not here." He smirked.

"I didn't think she would be, but it was worth a try. You know everything that goes on around here. Where is she?" I asked.

"Minnie got swept up into the system. She's got a warm place to sleep and real food to eat, not stale crackers and granola bars. Best to forget about her."

~

Minnie awoke in a bedroom with pale blue walls, starched lace curtains and sunlight pouring in through the windows. She had slept comfortably beneath a floral quilt. It looked like a setting out of a Hallmark movie. This was her room now that Mrs. Rutherford had found her and convinced her to come and live with her. Mrs. R. explained that she was the social worker assigned to her case when little Anna died. "When I found you at the homeless camp I felt that I owed you…something." She left out the part that she didn't accidentally find Minnie, she had tracked her down.

"I tried to find you and your husband after you left the hospital all those years ago. But Jim had put false information on the hospital admission form. That happens sometimes when people can't afford the bill. I'm not sure you were aware of that."

Minnie appeared confused. "No, I didn't know, but lying on the form didn't change anything. My baby still died." Minnie murmured with downcast eyes.

Helen didn't reply as she puttered about the kitchen, taking a carton of eggs from the refrigerator and setting a mixing bowl on the counter.

"How do you want your eggs?" Helen asked, changing the subject.

"Mrs. Rutherford, I told you I don't eat much. Maybe a piece of toast with butter and a cup of coffee. I haven't had toast or a good cup of coffee in a long time. You don't need to wait on me. Besides, I'm not used to eating a big meal in the morning. At the camp I unwrapped a granola bar and that was breakfast."

"Minnie, dear, call me Helen. And it's no trouble. No wonder you're so thin, well, we're going to change that." Helen was a woman on a mission and her mission was Minnie.

"Honestly," Minnie protested, "I don't understand all the fuss and why I'm even here. It's not that I'm not grateful. Your home is beautiful and you're very kind. But why did you bring me here? What do you want from me?" She was accustomed to blending in, a nameless, homeless person, and she preferred it that way.

"Oh, my dear, I don't want anything from you." Helen sat down next to Minnie and squeezed her hand. "It's what I can give to you—a second chance. You've had a hard life and I've been blessed with everything I need—and more. At my age I figure it's time to give back."

Minnie felt like Helen's 'pet project' and was determined to find a way out from under her watchful eye. Returning to the homeless camp was an option, not a pleasant one, but a return to what she was accustomed to. She thought about how she'd make her exit. For some reason Mrs. Rutherford felt she 'owed' Minnie something, but the feeling wasn't mutual.

~

"I can't forget about Minnie and I don't want to." I said.

"I could depend on Minnie for a steady supply of guns," Juan said. "Every week she'd show up with three, sometimes four guns in her backpack. She'd rummage through an unattended purse at the park while a mother pushed her kid on a swing or pretend to stumble over a backpack left on the floor at a fast-food joint. Homeless people are invisible. People look the other way. Minnie was my most reliable supplier."

"What happens to the guns?" I demanded.

"Everybody wants guns—criminals, government insurgents, stalkers, lunatics, mass murderers, revenge seekers. You name it. There's plenty of guns to go around. Those who can't get them legally will pay the price for a stolen weapon. Face it, that's how it is. Guns rule."

"Tell me how I can get in touch with her."

"You can't. She's severed all ties with the homeless. She may even have a new identity by now."

I turned to leave. Juan called after me. "Where do you think you're going?"

"I have a car waiting. I told her to call the police if I'm not back in a few minutes."

I ran, but Juan ran faster. He quickly caught up to me and twisted my arm behind my back, yanking it upward. "Stop it! You're hurting me!" I screamed.

"Then shut up and I'll go easy on you." He jabbed a gun into my ribs. "Keep quiet or I'll use this."

I stumbled along beside him as he dragged me to a battered black SUV and shoved me into the passenger seat, locked the door and hit the gas. The longer I was his captive and the further from the shelter he drove, the less likely that I'd be found—alive. I watched enough cop shows.

"I have to pee." I said, hoping to distract him. Even as a little kid stressful situations made me have to pee.

"You'll go when I tell you to, not before," he said jabbing the barrel into my ribs.

"That's not helping."

"Then shut up. We're almost there."

~

He stopped in the alley behind an abandoned building. Juan shuffled me inside and locked the door behind us. "Does this place have a bathroom?"

"Over there." He pointed around the corner with the gun.

The noxious odor from an unflushed toilet smacked me in the face. Disgusting. I pulled down my pants and squatted over the bowl, trying not to touch anything. I emptied my bladder and got the heck out of there.

"Jeez, Juan, this place is disgusting." I tried a friendly approach. No need to get him further riled up.

"What did you expect, the Four Seasons?" he snarled, pacing the floor.

"So now what?" I asked, realizing that I was hungry. I'd only had a cup of coffee all day and it was afternoon. Like my bladder, my stomach wasn't used to waiting.

"We wait." He mumbled.

"For what?" *More annoying questions from me?*

"You're a hostage, so we wait until they contact us."

"A hostage? What are you talking about? And who are *they*?" This was serious. More serious than collecting misplaced guns and handing them out to the homeless or selling them to thieves.

"Juan, it doesn't make sense. I don't have any money, my mother's dead and my father's missing. Who wants me as a hostage?"

"Just shut up. Shut up or I'll use this." He waved the gun menacingly in my direction. Juan was nervous and way out of his league. He was a petty thief, not a kidnapper.

"No, you won't," I retorted, "What good is a dead hostage?" I had no idea where this sudden outburst came from. I feared the unknown more than Juan and his gun. I was tired, hungry, and angry, caught up in something sinister and big. Big enough for someone to murder my mother and send my father into hiding. I didn't know who the bad guys were or how the pieces fit together, but I was determined to know the truth.

So, we waited. The storefront was dirty and musty. There were windows facing the alley. I got up to open one and let in some fresh air.

"What are you doing?" Juan snarled as he walked toward me.

"I just want to let some air in here!"

"Get over there and sit down. Now!" He shoved me, not enough to knock me down, but enough to assert his dominance. I sat until I couldn't sit still anymore. I paced for a while. What I really wanted to do was lay down and close my eyes, but not on the filthy floor. I had an idea. I arranged three folding chairs side-by-side to make a bench where I could stretch out.

"Hey, get me a couple of chairs while you're at it," Juan called over to me.

"Why should I?" I asked teasingly, trying to keep Juan in a good mood, even though he was holding me at gunpoint.

"Because I'm the one with the gun." He smirked and pointed it to the stacks of chairs. He sat down and put his feet up on a chair, appearing to settle in for the long haul. Deep down I didn't believe that Juan would kill me. Maybe rough me up, like before. It was a game of cat and mouse and I was the mouse.

I must have dozed off on my makeshift bed. I awoke to someone pounding on the back door yelling, "Open up."

Juan jumped up and peered through the grimy window. He unlocked the door and two burly guys stormed in brandishing automatic weapons.

"Where is she? Where's the girl?" they demanded.

"She's over there. Where's my money?"

I sat up. My pulse was racing. This was for real. Survivor instinct kicked in. I had no weapon. Escape was my only option, but before I could take a step toward the door one of the thugs grabbed my arm and yanked me toward him. "You're with me." He announced and dragged me toward the door. Juan was haggling with the other guy, demanding money.

"I want my money. I kept my side of the deal."

Gunfire exploded in the dim room. I screamed as Juan slumped against the wall.

"C'mon. Let's get the hell out of here. Get her in the van, now!" the shooter commanded.

A pasty-looking guy was waiting in the back of the van. He gagged me with a bandana and bound my hands and feet with duct tape. I'd seen enough movies to know not to panic. Keep your wits about you, although panicking seemed like a perfectly logical thing to do under the circumstances. I wished now that I hadn't left the apartment without telling Emma where I was going.

~

Emma stopped for groceries on her way home from work, planning to make a real dinner with salad and veggies instead of frozen pizza or ramen. She unlocked the door. The apartment was quiet. No television or radio. No Mia. She called Mia's name and checked the bedroom and bathroom, the only places she could possibly be in the tiny space. She realized that she'd made a mistake. She should never have left Mia alone after their argument last night. She immediately dialed Dick's number.

"Mia's not here. Everything is the same as when I left it this morning, minus Mia. Any idea where she might have gone?"

"No clue. I haven't exactly been father of the year, you know. What about that guy she's been hanging with? What's his name?"

"Debare, her boyfriend's name is Debare."

"Check him out. It's not like we can call the police."

~

The sky was dusky purple when Emma arrived at Debare's house. There were no cars in the driveway. The curtains were drawn and the house was dark except for a porch light. She rang the doorbell, no answer, then walked purposefully to the back as if she belonged there. She peered into the kitchen window. It was dinner time but the countertop and table were clear. There was no sign of life.

"She's not at Debare's house. The place looks deserted." Emma reported to Mia's father.

"Damn, you were supposed to be watching her! This is bad, Emma. Really bad. I have connections on the street. I'll see what I can find out. Keep looking—anywhere you think she might be."

~

I was held in a van with moving pads on the floor and hanging from the walls. It was dark and dusty in the windowless space. I could tell from the steady hum of the wheels that we were on a main road. We had stopped twice since leaving, probably at stoplights before getting on the freeway. I guessed we had been on the road for about twenty minutes, vital information to figure out how far from the homeless neighborhood they were taking me. I could make out the profile of the guy who bound and gagged me from the glare on his phone screen. I judged him to be in his twenties, chubby with curly red hair that fanned out around his head. He reminded me of a troll. I began making guttural noises and shaking my bound legs to get his attention. It worked.

"Shut up!" He seemed annoyed, but not vicious. At least he didn't hit me. I kept it up until he came over and untied the bandana.

"What?" he demanded.

"I have to pee." It was worth a try and by now I really did.

"Hold it!" He demanded. He didn't retie the gag. After a few minutes he called someone on his cellphone. "She says she had to pee." That was it. End of call.

He looked about the same age as Emma. There must be something I had in common with this guy, maybe music or favorite movies. I tried to start a conversation but he ignored me and told me to shut up. For the time being we were two people in the back of a van going God knew where. I was the mouse and he was the cat, a fat cat.

"Any idea where we're headed?" I asked.

"If I knew I sure as hell wouldn't tell you."

"I'm just asking. Don't get your shorts in a knot." I retorted with a phrase I'd heard my dad use. I decided to try another tack. "You know my mother was murdered and my dad is on the run, right?" He looked at me for the first time.

"Yeah, so what?"

"I was planning on going to college after I graduate, but now I'm not sure about anything. I'm staying with my murdered friend's sister. Everything is a mess." I said, trying to elicit sympathy. I had to get this guy on my side. I was relieved when he told me his story.

"After I graduated my dad lost his job so I had to stick around and help out at home." He tried to one-up me in the bad luck department. "Not what I'd planned for, either. Life's a bitch and then you die." He seemed resigned to his crappy life.

"I guess kidnapping innocent girls pays better than working behind a fast-food counter."

This struck a chord. He stiffened and retorted, "This is a one-off job and I'm done. Marco didn't tell me what was involved—just that after it was done I'd have a wad of cash and no one would get hurt if everyone did what they were told."

"So much for no one getting hurt. Your co-workers offed Juan in the blink of an eye. Just so you know, anyone that has anything to do with me ends up dead—my best friend Natalie, my mother, and now Juan. I'm jinxed, so you'd better watch your step."

"I'm terrified," he said without looking up from his phone.

We sat in silence for a while. The van slowed to a stop and the doors flung open.

"What's this? You took off her gag? Watch it, Louis, Marco won't stand for any slip- ups. If you know what I mean," the beefy guy said ominously. I shot a knowing look at Louis.

Juan unbound my legs and hands so I could pee in the bushes. I made Louis turn around and promise not to look. Everyone got back in the van and we were moving again, only this time it was on bumpy unpaved roads. I was startlingly hungry and thirsty and asked Louis if he was, too.

He grunted, "You won't starve." The miles ticked by in silence. The next time we stopped it was dusk. We parked in a clearing in the middle of a cornfield surrounded by endless rows of corn stalks. A thought popped into my head—there's got to be a farmhouse nearby with people and animals...and a phone. My brain was in overdrive. It's what I do best—overthink things.

One of the guys started a fire in a pit ringed by smooth rocks. My kidnappers must have used this spot before. A guy drove off in the van, hopefully to get some food. I felt lightheaded from hunger. It was completely dark when the van returned. The driver hopped out, distributing grease-stained sacs of fast food to everyone gathered around the fire. I was starving and devoured the fries, cheeseburger and apple pie slice. I'd never tasted beer, but that's all there was to drink so I washed down the greasy food with a can. With my belly full and my head buzzing from my first beer, all I wanted to do was sleep.

I stood up and started walking toward the van.

"Where do you think you're going?" Demanded Marco, the squat, head honcho. He reminded me of a fire hydrant. He was balding with a ruddy complexion and acne scars.

"To sleep—in the van," I replied. *Duh!*

"Not by yourself, you don't. Louis, go with her. And don't do anything I wouldn't do." he added with a leering smirk. Was he giving Louis permission to rape me? My stomach lurched from the greasy food, the beer and fear of what might happen. Marco called after us, "Keep an eye on her, Louis. If she escapes, you're a dead man, no questions asked."

"What's with that guy?" I asked when we were inside the van.

"He creeps me out, too. Like I said, this is a one-time job for me. I don't want to shoot anyone, so don't make me."

"What about the other thing, 'Don't do anything I wouldn't do?' What about that, huh?"

"Don't worry, just do as you're told and there won't be any trouble."

I made a nest of the moving pads and drifted into a fitful sleep. The van was as black as Marco's heart. I awoke with an achingly full bladder. It took me a few seconds to get my bearings.

"Louis," I called, softly at first, then louder until he roused. "I have to pee. I never drank beer before."

"Hold on," he said groggily. He illuminated his phone, stuck his gun in his waistband and unlatched the door. He turned his back and held the light over his shoulder as I walked a few rows into the corn and squatted.

While we walked back to the van I whispered, "We could run away right now. In the morning we'd both be gone and Marco would have no idea when or where."

"Are you crazy? You heard what he said. If you try to escape, I have to shoot you—I have no choice. Shut up and go back to sleep."

"Not if we escape together," I whispered. "I know you don't want to kill me." Those were the last works hanging in the air before the van was silent again.

I needed to work on Louis to get him to consider escaping with me. After seeing what happened to Juan after making good on his promise to kidnap me, I didn't have much hope for Louis. Was Marco really going to give Louis, a one-time newbie, a cut of the ransom? For the first time the idea of the ransom dawned on me; my life depended on Father paying a ransom. It was more than unsettling. Whatever sketchy 'business' my father ran could cost me my life. His secrecy about how he earned a living began to make sense. Whatever he was involved in was dangerous and illegal. I guessed it's what got my mother killed.

~

Emma thought it was strange that Juan wasn't lurking about when she set out to look for Mia at the homeless camp. Of course, no one would give any information to an outsider. Anyone she asked gave her a blank stare, shrugged their shoulders or mumbled about not knowing anything about anyone. Emma got back in her car and drove around the neighborhood. Cruising down a nearby alley she noticed that most of the shuttered storefronts were securely padlocked, so when she saw an open back door she decided to investigate. She called Mia's name as she entered through the alley door. No answer. She rounded a corner and gasped, covering her mouth. A body was slumped against the wall, surrounded by a pool of congealed blood and buzzing flies. It was Juan. She ventured further into the storefront calling Mia's name. On the floor next to a row of three chairs was Mia's backpack with her silver keychain attached to the zipper!

Emma bolted to the car and drove—fast. When she stopped trembling, she called Dick to report what she saw.

"They've got her, Dick! They've got Mia! She's in real danger! What are you going to do?"

"You mean, what are *we* going to do? You were supposed to look out for her and you dropped the ball!"

"Enough blame game. This is serious. Your daughter has been kidnapped! Don't you care?"

"Of course I care! She's my daughter, my only child."

"Have you heard from the kidnappers? Have they reached out to you?"

"No, because only you know where I am. I'll get word out that I'm ready to negotiate."

"Negotiate? Are you serious? This is your daughter! Are you willing to risk her life? Forget negotiating. Tell them you'll pay whatever!" A sudden jolt and the sound of metal grinding on metal forced the car into a sudden swerve. "Shit!"

"What? What's going on? Are you okay?"

"I just sideswiped a car. I'm fine. I wish I could say the same for Mia."

"I know it sounds cold, Emma, but that's how these things work. You just don't go out and pay them whatever they ask for. They expect negotiating." Dick said with authority. "Are you still there?"

"It sounds to me like you know way too much about kidnapping."

~

My first morning as a hostage we ate donuts and drank coffee around the firepit. After two donuts with sprinkles and a large coffee with two sugars I was on a sugar and caffeine high. One signal from Louis and I would have sprinted off into the cornstalks and not looked back.

Marco sat on a tree stump across from me and asked how my night was, again with the sleazy leer. With his five o'clock shadow and Friar Tuck hair he was truly repulsive. I vowed that if he tried anything I'd kick him in the balls and suffer the consequences. I sneered back at him which only made him laugh.

"I like a woman with spunk," he said.

"Go to hell." I replied. *You have no idea what I'm capable of, you creep!* The Mia that was taught to do as she was told and not to talk back was long gone. This was the new Mia.

Marco's dark, beady eyes scanned mine. I quickly looked away. "Your life depends on your father paying for your release," he said evenly, as if it was a simple business transaction. "It would be very beneficial—for you and me both—if you gave me his phone number. We can get this all cleared up in no time and you can go home to your cozy house in the burbs." He said sarcastically.

He knew nothing about me. He was trying to paint my life as cushy and normal when it was anything but. "First of all, Mr. Marco, I would love to go home to my cozy house in the burbs as you call it, but in case you've forgotten, you murdered my mother and now the house is a crime scene and my mother is in the morgue while the investigation continues. I don't know what illegal activity my father is involved in. I don't know how to contact him because my phone is in my backpack that was left at the crime scene where you murdered Juan." I took a breath. I don't know where I got the courage to blurt that rant to a murderous kidnapper who could kill me at his whim. I was beginning to realize that criminals weren't very smart, at least this bunch. Someone should have grabbed my backpack. I guess that would have fallen to Louis. Another mark against him, against him staying alive when this was over. Marco glared at Louis, who shrugged and mumbled something.

"What's your father's number?" Marco demanded.

"How should I know? Nobody under fifty memorizes phone numbers. It's in my phone that's in my backpack that's missing."

"Shut up you little brat! You'd better hope and pray that I can get in touch with your father." He removed his gun from his waistband and pointed it directly at my head. "As for your father, he's one of the biggest weapons traffickers in North America, shipping illegal firearms all over the world. You name it, he can get it. Anything from a tiny Derringer for a woman's purse to a rocket launcher. I asked politely for a share in his operation, a partnership, if you will, but he was greedy, wanted it all for himself. See where greed gets you? Remember that."

His words hit me hard, like a gut punch. My dad, a criminal? How could I have not known this? Did Mother know? It was beginning to make sense—his secrecy about his business, working long hours in his office. I wondered if Emma played a part in this.

"I've got people on the street looking for him," Marco said, "So if you know anything, you'd better tell us now. If I don't find him soon it doesn't look good for you."

An icy jolt shot down my spine. Marco's threat was real. I had to get in touch with my father and tell him that if he truly loved me, he needed to come up with the ransom money ASAP. I didn't know my father's phone number by memory. Why would I? But I did know Emma's. And Emma had a lot of explaining to do.

~

All the drama about finding my father aside, being held hostage was boring. No music, movies, internet, phone, bathroom facilities or decent food. Wherever I went, whatever I did, Louis shadowed me. If I took a short walk, Louis matched my stride. If I took a nap in the van—Louis was right there. I decided to make this work to my advantage. After another meal of greasy fast-food Louis accompanied me into the stalks for a bathroom break. Instead of going back to the camp immediately, I told Louis my plan.

"I'm worried, Louis. If they don't find my father—no ransom. If he doesn't come up with the cash, I'm dead—and so are you. You can identify Marco and his gang and with me gone there's no reason to keep you around. We both know too much."

His eyes narrowed. "Why are you telling me this?"

"I have a plan."

"Oh great, a plan." He hesitated for a moment. "Let's have it."

"My friend Emma is in contact with my father. I can call her and tell her about the ransom. But I don't want to put her in danger. That's why I didn't tell Marco about her."

I waited for this to sink in.

"I suppose you want me to call her." Louis finally spoke. "If Marco finds out I went behind his back, I'm dead. You know that."

"I think we're both dead, if we don't," I reasoned. Louis began walking back to the camp.

"We've been gone long enough. Marco will get suspicious."

I had to get in touch with Emma and Louis was my lifeline. I finally convinced Louis to call Emma on his phone. He dialed Emma's number, and as soon as it started to ring, I grabbed it from him. "Emma, it's me." Before I had a chance to explain she peppered me with a barrage of questions.

"Oh my God, Mia, where are you? Are you alright? I thought you might be...well, never mind. I've been looking everywhere for you. I went to *1929*, then to a storefront where I found your backpack—and a dead body."

"I'm in the middle of a cornfield—I can't talk long—I'm using my kidnapper's phone. My dad needs to pay the ransom for my release, now!"

"I knew you were in serious trouble," Emma said.

"Tell Dad the kidnappers are trying to reach him. The guy's name is Marco." Louis was signaling me to wrap it up. "I've got to go."

"Mia, wait!" Emma shouted, but Louis grabbed his phone and ended the call.

Another night sleeping in the van meant more crude remarks from Marco. Louis kept inching closer to me as I wrapped myself in what felt like the security of the moving pads. "What the heck, Louis?" I hissed at him. "There's a whole van here. Back off." I wanted to establish boundaries without putting Louis off completely. I considered him an ally and under different circumstances he might have been a friend. Louis was a good guy, that's what my gut told me and my gut was usually right. I believed that he would try to protect me if it came to that. But the clock was ticking and Marco would only wait so long for my father to come up with the ransom. I had to act fast. Louis was the key to my escape.

"I'm just trying to keep you safe. I wouldn't put it past those guys out there to...well, you know, take advantage," Louis stammered. I thought it was sweet that he was protecting my honor, but I needed more from him.

"Thanks, Louis, but what I really need is to get the heck out of here before Marco loses his patience and does something stupid. It's got to be soon. I don't trust him at all."

I spent the day planning our escape; that night in the van I'd say I had to pee and Louis and I would make a break for it through the stalks. Maybe a farmer lived nearby and we could hide in his barn. Perhaps the smooth river rocks around the campfire meant that there was a stream or river in the area that we could follow. A lot of maybes.

I was grasping at straws but I wasn't waiting around for Marco to act first.

When I shared the plan with Louis, he looked at me as if I was insane. "Once Marco sees that I'm missing, your life is worthless," I explained. "Louis, let me ask you something. Have you ever seen a dead body?"

He hesitated.

"Well, I've seen my best friend *and* my mother ambushed and murdered with firearms. Forget the bullshit the government feeds us about handguns keeping us safe, it's a lie. I'm a survivor and I'm planning to remain among the living until I can finish high school and college, have a career, and maybe get married and have kids."

Louis shook his head. "You've got your life all planned out. I wish I knew what the hell I was going to do after this." Louis mused.

"This is my plan. If you have a better one, let me know." He grunted. I took it as his consent. It was settled.

That night, not surprisingly, I couldn't sleep. When the camp was quiet, I rousted Louis who never seemed to have trouble sleeping.

"This is it. Time to go." But when he attempted to open the van doors, they were locked from the outside! Did Marco know about my plan? How could he? Did Louis tell him? I couldn't let myself believe that. I thought Louis was on my side.

"Now what?" Louis wanted to know.

"Let me think." By now I really did have to pee. I began pounding on the walls and yelling. Eventually, one of the kidnappers unlocked the door and stuck his head in, cursing and asking what all the noise was about.

"Why are the doors locked? Do you want me to wake you up every time I have to pee?" I asked.

When we returned to the van Louis convinced him not to lock us in again. After waiting for what seemed like hours, I quietly opened the door and listened. All I could hear was the wind rustling the leafy cornstalks and violent snoring. Louis was peacefully sleeping. *Should I wake him or strike out on my own?* I gently lifted the moving pad searching for his gun. He suddenly grabbed my arm. "What's going on?" he demanded.

"Louis, if we're going to do this we've got to go now. Are you with me?" He relaxed his grasp on my arm, groaned and turned over.

"Jesus, can't you just let me sleep?"

"I was going to—but now you're awake and time is running out. Come on!"

The night air was cool and damp with eerie ground fog. We disappeared into the tall cornrows, slowly at first so as not to rustle the leaves, then sprinting when we were a safe distance away. The razor-sharp leaves sliced my arms and legs, drawing blood. I ran as fast as I could for as long as I could until a side splint forced me to stop. I doubled over, gasping for breath. We waited until I caught my breath then set off again.

It seemed like we ran forever, stopping briefly to rest then continuing. The night sky gradually brightened, birds chattered and chirped. We pressed on, stopping occasionally, not sure where we were going. Eventually the sun rose above the stalks melting the morning mist.

Where to now?

~

Again, I stopped to catch my breath and stood still, my head cocked, listening. Louis gave me a quizzical look.

"Do you hear that?" I whispered.

"Hear what?" he replied.

"Shh." I put my finger to my lips. "Listen." We were momentarily silent. "The highway. We're near the interstate! It's our ticket out of here! Let's go."

But instead of moving along the corn rows as we had been, we now walked through the stalks, parting them with our hands that soon became bloodied and raw. We stopped occasionally to make sure we were headed toward the highway—and freedom. The sun was overhead now. We swatted pesky insects mercilessly attacking our sweating, bleeding bodies. A crust caked the corners of my parched lips. The hum of traffic grew louder.

Suddenly we burst out of the cornfield, separated from the highway by a drainage ditch filled with stagnant water, reeds, and trash. We half-sprinted, half-tumbled down a steep embankment to the edge of the ditch.

I nudged Louis. "You first. Watch out for snakes."

"Thanks," he said as he waded into the murky water. "Come on in, the water's fine," he laughed, gingerly making his way up the opposite embankment.

The mud sucked at my shoes as I scurried across, slipping up the muddy embankment until I reached the shoulder of the highway. Without wasting any time, I began waving my arms and shouting. Cars and trucks sped by. Some slowed to look. No one stopped. After a while I sat down in the grass, my head on my arms.

"This isn't working," I mumbled. I was hungry, thirsty, tired and on the verge of tears, but we couldn't give up now. We'd made it this far.

Louis paced, a worried look on his face. "Let's just keep walking."

"Which way?" I asked.

"With traffic, I guess," he said with a shrug. "At least we'll feel like we're headed somewhere."

We began walking backward, our thumbs out, shoes squishing with every step. Our damp, dirty clothes clung to our sweaty bodies. Walking backward was exhausting, but we trudged along, hoping someone would pull over and give this motley pair a lift.

~

Minnie was suffocating under Mrs. Rutherford's watchful eye. She was always annoyingly cheerful which pressured Minnie to act the same. But it was just an act while she planned her escape. Minnie concocted an elaborate story; she had a cousin 'out east' that she had contacted and was invited to come and stay—permanently, no strings attached. She would finally get out from under Mrs. Rutherford's thumb then secretly return to 1929 and anonymity. When she finally got the nerve to bring it up one evening after dinner, Mrs. R would have none of it.

"But my dear, you simply cannot travel thousands of miles to live with a distant relative who may not have the means to support you. No, I won't hear of it. Besides, there's something I've wanted to tell you since I found you at the homeless camp.

"Losing your Anna was the worst thing imaginable. But what would you say if I told you that it was all a mistake?"

Minnie frowned. "What do you mean, it was all a mistake? What are you saying?"

"Brace yourself for a shock. A happy one, but a shock all the same."

"A shock, what kind of shock?"

"Your Anna is alive."

Minnie clutched her chest, tears welling. "After all these years? Is this a cruel joke? Why are you doing this to an old woman? Jim and I took Anna to the emergency room. They said she died of pneumonia. If only we'd brought her sooner…" She sobbed into her gnarled hands. "Now you're saying she's been alive all these years. I don't believe you! You're lying, it isn't true!"

"Minnie, she didn't die. Her organs had shut down, but she wasn't dead. When a nurse was about to bring her tiny body to the morgue, she saw movement and revived her. Anna survived! Like you, she's a survivor!"

Stunned, Minnie tried to process this news. Between sobs of happiness she blurted, "But how do you know all this? Why didn't you tell us? Everything would have been different! Jim wouldn't have left, and I wouldn't be homeless. Why now?"

"Everyone was trying to find you, but you had already left the hospital and with the fake address on the admission form, we assumed that you didn't *want* to be found."

Minnie wiped her eyes with her sleeve and looked intently at Helen. "If what you're saying is true, I want to see her. I want to see my daughter."

"She was adopted by a family who loved and cared for her. I know this because I was the social worker who arranged the adoption. When I saw your name on a recent list of homeless clients with outstanding medical bills, I did some research and discovered that you are Anna's mother. I was determined to make amends for my mistake."

"Mistake?"

"I should have done more to find you and your husband. I was young and eager to place Anna in a good home. Believe me when I tell you that Anna was well cared for. I saw to it."

"You had no right!" Minnie's face crumpled. "She must think that Jim and I abandoned her. I want to see her! I want her to know the truth—that we were heartbroken at losing her."

Suddenly it all began to make sense. Helen didn't look for her out of a genuine desire to help, it was out of *guilt*. For years Helen's conscience tormented her. Minnie pushed her plate away and trudged up the stairs, overwhelmed with the news. Closing the bedroom door, she collapsed onto the bed, crying, trying to make sense of everything. One thing was certain—she would find her daughter, with or without Helen's help.

~

As we walked along the shoulder, dodging broken glass, shredded tires and roadkill, I knew that Marco and his crew were frantically searching for us. If they saw us hitchhiking, they could easily run us over and claim it was an accident. With every approaching vehicle my pulse quickened. The next one could be the white van with Marco and his crew inside. I waved my fist at one trucker who laid on his air horn a few feet away from us but didn't stop. My hair was slick with sweat. I couldn't walk another step.

I plopped down in the gravel and sobbed. Louis squatted next to me. "I know it sucks but we have to keep moving." His eyes were on the road. He was also looking for the white van. "Come on." He helped me up and we continued walking.

I trudged along robotically, trying to shut out my fear and hunger. Late in the afternoon a tractor trailer slowed down and pulled over. With our last ounce of strength, we ran toward the red cab.

The driver wore a tattered ball cap, on top of and several days of salt and pepper stubble and a complexion like tanned leather. "Where y'all headed?"

Louis and I looked at each other. We hadn't had time to come up with a cover story. *Where were we headed?* We had no idea. Before he lost interest and pulled away, I blurted, "Kennison."

"Well, that's where I'm headed, too. Climb in. My handle's Twitch."

Twitch talked non-stop, happy to have someone to listen to his stories about life on the road and back home where he and his wife raised Pit Bulls. I was too exhausted to pay attention. I was hungry and thirsty and Louis was too, although he didn't complain. Finally, after listening to my stomach growl, Twitch asked, "When's the last time you two ate anything?"

"Yesterday," I admitted.

"Well, we can't have that, now can we?"

He pulled over at the next truck stop, a beehive of activity with families vacationing in their RVs and truckers stopping for a meal and rest from the long-haul. I used the restroom and splashed cold water on my grimy face and arms. I hoped that Louis had enough cash to pay for chips, granola bars and juice—a feast and the healthiest food I'd eaten in days. I began peeling the wrapper off a protein bar and guzzled grape juice to wash it down. We scanned the parking lot for Marco's white van. All clear. We bolted for the rig.

"We're good," I announced, climbing up into the cab. "Let's go." Twitch gave me a strange look as he fired up the engine.

"You two okay? It's none of my business, but I've got a radio if y'all need help."

"We're fine." I lied, tearing into a bag of salty chips. Calling the police might save me, but it would put Dad in danger. Not only did the police want to question him about Mother's murder, but his illegal business activities meant the feds were involved, too. I didn't want to be the one responsible for sending my only living parent to prison.

Greasy, salty potato chips never tasted so delicious. I was busy munching when Twitch announced that a white van was tailing us and he couldn't shake it. I looked in the mirror, and sure enough, Marco's white van was close behind. Twitch slowed down and sped up but he couldn't shake the van.

"Do y'all know them?"

"Yeah," Louis and I responded in unison.

"It's a long story," I said, "but we definitely need to ditch them."

Twitch got on his CB radio and alerted his trucker buddies that he needed help. As he did, Marco pulled up alongside the rig. The guy in the passenger seat pointed a gun at Twitch, yelling at him to pull over. When he didn't, the guy started shooting. Louis and I ducked. Twitch leaned away from the window, struggling to retrieve his gun from under the seat while trying to avoid a fiery crash. The truck swerved violently. I was certain we'd end up in a ditch. Gunshots shattered the window. Nobody was hit, but Marco clearly meant business.

Minutes later, a caravan of trucks, old and new, surrounded Twitch's rig forcing the van onto the shoulder. We didn't see Marco's white van after that.

Despite Twitch's CB chatter and blaring country music, Louis and I fell asleep, more like passed out, as the truck roared along. We were awakened by the hiss of air brakes as the rig turned into a busy truck stop on the outskirts of Kennison.

"I'm taking the by-pass, so let me know if you want out here." Twitch announced. "Listen, I don't know what you kids are involved in but be careful." We thanked him and assured him that we would.

What choice did we have? We headed inside the crowded truck stop where computer stations were available for a small fee. I punched in Emma's number and clicked on a face-to-face call. It took a while before Emma appeared on the screen.

"Oh My God! Mia! Are you alright? You look like hell!" She was wearing a grey hoodie, her hair was a tangled mess and she had dark circles under her eyes. I was inwardly glad that she was losing sleep over my disappearance. I didn't know what part, if any, she played in my father's weapons business, but I was certain they were together, even before my mother was murdered. For that I would never forgive her. But now I needed her help. She owed me, big time.

I explained how I went to 1929 to search for Minnie and ended up kidnapped and forced into a van.

"We're at the truck stop outside Kennison. The big one off the interstate."

"Who's with you?" she asked.

"Louis, one of my kidnappers."

"Why is he letting you call me? I'm confused."

"Louis and I escaped. Marco and his gang shot up the rig we hitched a ride in, but Twitch ditched them. We're safe, for now, but we need to get out of here. It's only a matter of time before they catch up to us."

"Who the hell is Twitch?" Emma demanded.

"It's a long story. I'll tell you the details when you get here. And Emma—hurry!

~

After Minnie found out that Anna was alive, her mood shifted wildly between elation and despair. She was relieved that her daughter was alive, raised in a good home and wanted for nothing. Bouts of regret snuffed out her happiness. Minnie never got to experience the joy and pain of raising her only child. What lies had Anna been told about her adoption? Did she think that her birth mother had given her up for adoption or abandoned her? Was she told that Minnie had died in childbirth?

With Anna in their lives, she and Jim would have stayed together, a happy little family struggling to make ends meet. Minnie understood that Helen's reason for plucking her from the homeless camp was to ease her guilty conscience. How could she have lived all with herself all these years knowing that she had caused so much pain and destroyed Minnie's family?

In the days that followed, as Minnie became increasingly taciturn, Helen ramped up her efforts to appease her. "How about a day of shopping, and a spa visit for manicures, massages and new hairdos? I know I could use a makeover," Helen admitted.

Minnie would have none of it. "I want to see my daughter," was all she would say.

During the adoption process, Helen hadn't been entirely truthful with Anna's adoptive parents. She insisted that she was unable to contact Anna's birth parents, letting them believe that Minnie and Jim had abandoned her. She glossed over the fact that she had only made minimal attempts to find them before proceeding with the adoption. It was a dark secret that she had carried with her for a long time. Too long.

When she dug deeper, Helen admitted to herself that she had overstepped her boundaries as a social worker, taking matters into her own hands. Wouldn't little Anna be better off, Helen reasoned, in a home with educated, middle-class parents who would provide her with a good education and every material thing she needed or wanted? Wasn't this better for the sickly child than poor, uneducated parents who couldn't even afford medical care? Helen had made her decision and wasted no time acting on it. She was friends with the judges in family court and they trusted her judgement. If Helen Rutherford couldn't find little Anna's parents, then nobody could in their estimation. But Helen knew it wasn't true. She wanted to be a hero, the social worker who kept Anna out of the sticky web of the foster care system.

~

Emma pulled her tangled hair into a messy ponytail. She slipped into flip-flops and didn't bother changing out of her hoodie and leggings. *I look like hell, but Mia needs me.* She squealed out of the driveway before slowing to ten miles over the speed limit. *Don't risk getting pulled over. Just go with the flow of traffic. Don't draw attention.* She couldn't identify the kidnappers, but maybe they were already on to her.

Emma pulled into the truck stop. From inside Mia spotted Emma and scanned the lot for any sign of the white van, then opened the door. She and Louis sprinted to Emma's car.

"Let's go." Mia commanded. "I'll explain everything on the way."

"Where are we going?" Emma asked. "And who's your friend?"

"To your apartment, I guess." Mia said. "This is Louis," She nodded toward the backseat. "He helped me escape."

"Oh," Emma checked Louis out in the rearview mirror. Sweaty and dirty, his hair was a bushy red halo.

"If Marco finds us, he'll kill Louis for letting me escape. Right, Louis?" He nodded while searching out the window for any sign of Marco's white van. "I figure I'm more valuable alive than dead. That's if Dad comes up with the ransom."

Emma drove slower than her usual pedal to the metal style. Best not to get pulled over with two escapees and a fugitive's girlfriend. Mia and her father's photo were all over the internet and on local news. If the police found Mia, Marco would forfeit the ransom, a death sentence for her father.

"The problem is that Marco still hasn't contacted your dad for the money drop. Dick's trying to reach out to him through his street contacts. He knows it's the only way to keep you safe." Emma said as she took the exit toward her apartment.

Louis spoke his first words since entering the car, "I think I know a way that we can save everyone's skin— Mia's, her dad's and mine."

Mia turned to look at Louis then shrugged. "I've got nothing. Out with it!"

"I'll call Marco and tell him that you are still my prisoner, that I caught up to you while you were trying to escape. Score one for me. Then I tell him that I have a connection to your father. More points for me. Marco sets up the money drop. Your dad doesn't even have to be there. Emma can bring the money. The switch is complete—ransom money for Mia's freedom—everyone's happy."

"There's one problem. A big one." Emma said. "We don't know how much money Marco is demanding and I don't know if Dick can get his hands on a large amount of cash at short notice. He's in hiding. It's not like he can go to the bank and withdraw money. The police are surely keeping a close eye on all his accounts. They'll grab him if he tries to make a cash withdrawal."

"He doesn't have to. He can do it online." Louis offered.

"You've really thought this out." Emma replied, surprised at his initiative.

"Survivor instinct." Louis said. "I'm out to save my own skin, too."

We followed Emma up the stairs to her apartment. After a shower and a change of clothes, I announced that I was starving and Louis chimed in that he was, too. Emma gave Louis a change of clothes that I recognized as my father's shirt and sweatpants.

"The proverbial cupboard is bare," Emma said staring at a cabinet with a box of crackers, a can of soup and a jar of stuffed olives. "You good with pizza?' She phoned in the order then sat down next to me on the sofa. "You've been through so much." She gave me a hug. "What's our next move?"

"Sorry, Emma. I'm so hungry I can't think straight. Can it wait until later?" I grabbed a slightly wrinkled apple from a bowl on the countertop and gobbled it down while Louis munched on the crackers and watched a ball game on TV.

I must have dozed off. The buzzer startled me awake. Emma paid the pizza driver and was about to close the door when two guys brandishing guns pushed past Emma and slammed the door. It was Marco and one of his burly henchmen.

"How did you find us?" I blurted. I foolishly thought Louis and I were finally free.

"You didn't think I'd forgotten about you?" Marco said with his usual sneer. "We followed you and were about to bust the door down when the pizza guy did our work for us. No muss no fuss." Marco turned his attention to Louis who was cowering in the corner. "And you…" He waved his weapon menacingly, "I should do you right here and now, but I don't want the neighbors calling the police. I've got a boatload of cash due me and I'm not leaving without it." So much for Louis's plan. Clearly, I wasn't his prisoner.

"It's not his fault," I nodded toward Louis, "I made Louis leave with me. It was the only way I could contact my dad, get the ransom and save myself. You should be thanking him."

"Oh, that's rich. I should be thanking him because he let you escape? I don't think so. I'll deal with him later. Let's get down to business, the reason I'm here—the ransom. Get your dad on the phone—now."

"You keep forgetting, I don't have a phone, thanks to you."

"I don't care whose phone you use, just call him, NOW!" Emma and I both jumped. Louis looked like he was about to cry.

"I'll call him," Emma said. "He'll only answer my calls, anyway."

When Dad answered, Marco grabbed the phone from Emma. "I've got your daughter and if you want to see her alive, I need $500K in twenty-four hours."

"Not so fast. Let me talk to her." Dad said. Marco handed me the phone.

"Dad, it's me, I'm alright, but please, get the money." Marco quickly grabbed the phone.

"Satisfied? You'll hear from me tomorrow." Marco ended the call and put the phone in his pocket. "I'm in charge, now. You got any beer?"

Emma and I looked at each other with disbelief. I had escaped the camp, but I was still Marco's prisoner, and now Emma was, too. I hoped that Dad could scrape together that kind of cash in a day. If not, well, I didn't want to think about the consequences. I'd already seen what had happened to Juan. I knew perfectly well what Marco was capable of.

~

The harder Helen tried to bond with Minnie, the more she resisted. Minnie decided that the only way she could find peace was to speak with Anna herself, face to face, to try to convince her that she hadn't abandoned her. If Helen wouldn't help her, then she would do it on her own. She was prepared to overcome any obstacle to reconnect with her daughter, the daughter lost to her thanks to Helen's need for power and control. Besides, Minnie thought, what more could possibly happen? She'd already lost everything dear to her. She had nothing more to lose.

Minnie had rejected Helen's offers of new clothes and a makeover, but she began to reconsider. Why not take advantage of the gifts Helen offered? If she looked less like a homeless woman and more like a someone that Anna could relate to, Minnie reasoned, it might improve her chances of forming a relationship. They never had a chance to form a mother-daughter bond, their time together was so short, only a few months. When they were separated, Anna was only an infant, too young to have any memory of her birth mother; no mental image, no memory of lullabies sung while she snuggled in her mother's arms, most importantly, no memory of her mother's touch.

Minnie's quest for self-improvement was not only to look like a woman Anna would want to get to know, but for Minnie to feel worthy of her beautiful, educated daughter, a high-powered attorney in the nation's capital. Minnie searched hungrily for information about her daughter and found that she did more than her firm's required pro-bono work. One local newspaper called her "a champion" for the homeless. Minnie recognized the irony.

Minnie, who had never traveled more than fifty miles from Kennison, would have to go to the capitol, seven hundred miles away. She had never been on an airplane or a train, but she had taken a bus once to visit an ailing aunt in a nearby town. She had so much to learn, and so many plans to make. She decided to take it one step at a time. First, she would work on her appearance. While she had previously rejected Helen's offers, she warmed to the idea and accepted Helen's invitation to a spa day.

Minnie marveled at the modern salon, shiny sharp angles and bright lights. Worlds away from her annual trip to the barber shop with her father to get her hair cut short for the summer. At the homeless camp the women cut each other's hair, sometimes with disastrous results.

Her neck ached as it hung over the rim of the shampoo sink, but the scalp massage felt amazing. Then it was on to the colorist who suggested that Minnie get rid of the grey and bring back her pale blonde color with natural highlights. Minnie laughed at herself in the mirror. She looked like an alien with rows of aluminum foil folded over strands of hair to achieve a 'natural look.'

Afterward, the stylist asked about the cut. Minnie had always wanted a short cut that would emphasize her cheekbones and hazel eyes. When the stylist finished, she handed Minnie a mirror and turned the chair around so she could see the back. Minnie's lips parted with a wide, toothy grin. It was hard to believe that her brittle, dull hair was now sleek and stylish. Last on the agenda was a manicure and pedicure. Minnie was overwhelmed by the number of colors. In the end she selected shell pink. When the spa day was over she was grateful to Helen, but she stayed focused on her mission to reunite with her daughter.

There seemed no end to the perks that Helen offered, like dangling a carrot on a stick. Minnie wondered what the final payoff was for Helen. What did she want? Minnie would take advantage of everything that Helen offered then make her exit, with or without Helen's blessing.

Next, Helen arranged medical appointments; physical, dental, and eye exams. Turned out, Minnie needed bifocals and chose a pair of tortoise shell frames that complimented her heart-shaped face and new hair style. A young female doctor told Minnie that she was underweight and recommended a diet of fresh fruits and vegetables, poultry, fish and occasional red meat, along with a daily multivitamin with iron.

Minnie couldn't remember the last time she had seen a dentist. She needed extensive work to replace missing teeth and repair cavities. She hesitated when asked to sign a waiver saying that she was responsible for the cost because she knew that she had no way to pay. When Helen intervened and signed her name as the responsible party, Minnie breathed a sigh of relief. She wondered if Helen wanted her to feel obligated, but Minnie hadn't asked for any of this and didn't feel that she owed Helen anything. Helen owed Minnie much more than she could ever repay, Minnie's lost time with her daughter.

Minnie's wardrobe consisted of thrift store finds and charity donations. When you're homeless it doesn't matter what you wear. She didn't need to dress for work because hadn't had a real job in years. The last one she could remember required a store uniform. When she turned in weapons to Juan he gave her a small cash payment, but it wasn't enough to live on and it wasn't consistent. It was almost impossible for a homeless person to hold down a job. She didn't own an alarm clock, appropriate clothes, a phone, or access to reliable transportation.

If Minnie intended to find a job she needed appropriate clothes to wear to an interview. Even though Helen was footing the bill, Minnie didn't want or need anything fancy. She selected slacks, blouses, underwear, socks, shoes, and pajamas. Her old sweatshirts, worn blue jeans and men's crew socks went into the trash. After a day of shopping, Minnie's new wardrobe filled several shopping bags. Exhausted, she headed upstairs to rest and dream about meeting Anna. She realized that she didn't know what Anna looked like since she last saw her as a fragile infant, struggling to breathe. She longed to see her baby pictures, classroom photos, Anna at the beach, on a picnic, perhaps team photos or a school play. She asked Helen for photos of her daughter as a child, a childhood that she knew nothing about.

Minnie insisted on helping Helen around the house. She did her share of cooking, cleaning, taking out the trash and other household chores. She thought it was only fair that she contribute. Having a washer and dryer in the house without having to trek to the laundromat with a pillowcase full of soiled laundry and a pocketful of change was nothing short of a miracle. She enjoyed all the comforts that Helen provided knowing she could never repay her.

At breakfast Helen offered a variety foods to help Minnie gain weight: eggs, toast, bagels with cream cheese, bacon, and croissants with jam. It awakened a feeling in Minnie that had been missing for a long time—gratitude. While the favors were appreciated, she couldn't stop wondering. What did Helen want in return? There had to be something. A promise from Minnie to keep the circumstances of Anna's quick adoption a secret? The more Minnie thought about it, the more she realized that she wielded tremendous power over Helen—a secret that could destroy her credibility, her career, and possibly threaten her freedom.

~

We were helpless. The only thing Emma, Louis and I could do was wait—wait for Dad to carry out Marco's instructions about when and where to drop the cash. *Go alone. Put the money in an army surplus duffle bag. Follow the directions exactly or you'll never see your daughter alive.*

Like a scene from a movie, but terrifyingly real. I tried to stay positive, but I couldn't help imagining everything that could go wrong.

I resented the idea of having to be rescued, even by my father. I'd managed to escape once. If this deal went sour, I'd do it again. When would this nightmare end? When could I get on with my life, a life that had barely begun? Could Dad raise that kind of cash on short notice? I had no way of knowing. My life was at the mercy of two men; one whom I loved and one I hated.

If Dad couldn't raise the cash that Marco demanded, I'd have to have a Plan B. Now was the time to cobble one together. Emma and I retreated to the bedroom and locked the door. Seconds later, Marco's goon pounded demanding that we 'open up.' *Jeez, can't a girl have some privacy?* How could we plan our escape if we couldn't talk without someone eavesdropping? We needed a code, but how to invent one on the spur of the moment? We could pass notes like in school, but not with the beastly boy peering in at us every few minutes. I lay across the bed, my hands propped under my chin, thinking. Then it came to me—Scrabble! We'd spell out our plan using Scrabble letters. I doubted that Marco's beefy henchman was familiar with the game or would suspect what we were up to.

We set up the Scrabble board, drew letters to see who would go first, wrote our names on the top of the score sheet and drew letters, lots of letters. Not the seven required for the game. We spelled out phrases like, *how much time? Where to go? How to get there?*

I was correct. The dude was clueless. He assumed we were playing a harmless board game. Through trial-and-error Emma and I came up with a plan. The best time to act, we decided, was when Marco went to retrieve the money. Someone had to stay behind to guard us. It would be three against one, good odds under any circumstances. That is, if Louis really was on our side and not bluffing until the last second when he might turn on Emma and me.

~

The next morning Marco got up early and made a racket opening the refrigerator and banging cabinet doors looking for something to eat. To his credit, he made a pot of coffee. Emma and I straggled out of bed for a cup, black, since there wasn't any cream or sugar, just some old packets of cancer-causing sweetener that Marco added to his coffee. Unfortunately, it would take years for it to take effect.

"What? Are you on a diet?" Marco bellowed. "There's not a damn thing to eat! AJ, go find a donut place and get a couple dozen." He handed AJ some cash. It looked like our breakfast would consist of sugar and caffeine. Great. We'd all be hyped up. At least neither side had an advantage. Before AJ left I asked if he could also get some orange juice. He rolled his eyes and grunted. I hoped that meant yes.

Marco hunkered down on the sofa watching the news. A photo of my dad, clean-shaven, appeared on the screen. Probably from his driver's license. Marco sat upright. "I wouldn't want to be in his shoes." Underneath the photo a banner scrawled. *If you see this man, call your local police. He is wanted on suspicion of murder and illegal weapons trafficking.*

A photo of me as a freshman at New Hope Academy, flashed on the screen. 'Missing' in red letters beneath it and a phone number to call if I was seen. I hadn't been to school in days. Apparently, Emma hadn't called in my absence. Not that it would have mattered.

~

Minnie discovered that with a new outfit and hairstyle she was actually welcomed at the local library, unlike the frosty and sometimes rude reception she got when she was homeless. Libraries were favorite hangouts for the unhoused. It was a great place to spend the day, especially if it was hot outside, but if you fell asleep, you'd be asked to leave. Once an insensitive librarian had sprayed Minnie with Lysol when she was browsing through the magazines on an exceptionally hot, humid day. The indignity brought tears to her eyes, not to mention the spray itself, but she quickly dried her eyes and regained her composure. She would not give that bitchy librarian the satisfaction of seeing her cry. When she returned to the homeless camp, a long-time resident told her that the librarian could be charged with assault and battery for spraying her against her will. *What were the chances of that?* Minnie knew from experience that folks like her were either invisible or thrown to the curb, their rights trampled because they had no voice. Now the tables were turned and the librarian behind the desk, Roberta, greeted her with a smile and offered to help her find what she was looking for.

Minnie intended to book a trip to the capitol, where Anna lived. She'd never learned to drive and was terrified at the prospect of flying. That left either a train or a bus. She didn't have a phone and was completely befuddled as to how computers worked. She dare not ask Helen for help, who adamantly claimed that Anna wanted nothing to do with her. But Minnie had doubts about that. Maybe it was because Helen was afraid that Minnie would tell her the truth about her adoption. Minnie approached the librarian, uncertain as to how to begin planning her trip.

"Hi. I'm not familiar with computers. I'm trying to book a trip to visit my daughter. Can you help me, please?"

"Of course, I can certainly help you with that." Minnie shared that she didn't have a computer or a cell phone and that she was terrified of flying. Minnie let her guard down, mentioning that she hadn't seen her daughter in many years and was very excited about the trip.

"I can print out the bus and train schedules for you. If you're not familiar with computers you can order the tickets by phone." Roberta said. "You'll need a credit card."

Shoulders slumping, Minnie sighed. "Okay, I'll do that," forcing a smile.

Minnie turned to leave, discouraged but not defeated. She had no money, job or credit card but she was determined to visit Anna without Helen's knowledge or help.

~

Emma and I waited nervously for AJ to come back with the donuts and juice. My stomach was growling and I felt lightheaded. The second he arrived, we all descended on the box of donuts and ate ravenously. I asked AJ to pass the orange juice but changed my mind after he opened the container and took a swig. God, what a Neanderthal—no offense to Neanderthals.

"I hope your father scraped together the 500K." Marco looked directly at me as he stuffed his Smith and Wesson into his waistband.

Without warning, all my fear and anxiety bubbled to the surface, a tidal wave of emotion. I thought I'd kept it under wraps, but I was only kidding myself. I was terrified. I cried like a toddler separated from her mother for the first time. I was inconsolable. It started with a quivering chin, a few hiccups, then a deluge of sobs and tears that I couldn't stop. The loss of Natalie, my mother, my freedom, and not the least of which, Debare's absence overwhelmed me. Disgusted, Marco told Louis to shut me up or get me the hell out of there.

Louis took me out to the tiny balcony overlooking the parking lot and closed the sliding door behind us. I buried my face into his chest and tried to imagine he was Debare. He didn't smell like Debare, wasn't muscular like Debare, and certainly wasn't handsome like Debare. To Louis's credit, he hugged me while I wailed and declared how unfair it all was. My best friend and my mother were dead, my father was a criminal, and my life hung by a thread. After I'd cried myself out, I was exhausted and felt utterly defeated. We went back inside. Marco and AJ were gone. Emma was on the sofa watching television.

"Where'd everyone go?' I asked, wiping snot with my sleeve.

"Marco went to collect the ransom. AJ must have gone with him." Emma said.

I suddenly snapped to attention. "They left us alone? This is our chance. Let's get as far away from here as possible before they get back." No one moved. "What are we waiting for? Let's go!"

"I'm willing to take my chances here." Emma said. "Marco promised to let us go once he had the money."

"And you believe him?" What was Emma thinking? Had she forgotten about the plan we made last night? "Listen to me, I've seen what Marco is capable of. We are all expendable. Every one of us. Especially me and Louis."

"It's *you* they want, not me." Emma said. "I'm safer if I stay put. I'll say I tried to stop you but you overpowered me."

"Well, I'm not waiting around. I'm out of here." I announced. I didn't have anything to take with me, just the clothes I was wearing. I carefully opened the apartment door and peered into the hallway. Next to the elevator, AJ was smoking a cigarette. I quickly closed the door and retreated inside the apartment.

"We're not alone. AJs in the hallway having a smoke. Quick, before he comes back, help me over the balcony," I said.

"What are you doing? If AJ comes back while you're dangling over the railing, you're dead for sure." Emma said.

"I'll help you, kid," Louis offered, glancing at Emma and shaking his head.

Luckily, we were on the second floor. I climbed over the railing and Louis lowered me down to the thick shrubs below. Once I was on solid ground, I motioned for him to follow.

~

At dinner that night, Minnie told Helen that she wanted to get a job to save money for a place of her own.

"Do you have any marketable skills, dear?" Helen asked, barely hiding the condescension in her voice, eager to dismiss Minnie's plan.

"I don't have any office skills, but I can reshelve books at the library. I saw a notice posted on the bulletin board there today."

"How will you get there? You don't drive," Helen reminded her.

"I've taken the bus my entire life and I don't see any reason to stop now," Minnie responded with confidence.

"Well, dear, if that's what you want," Helen replied, in her smug manner. She didn't believe that Minnie could get or keep a job, but Minnie was determined to prove her wrong.

Minnie's librarian friend Roberta helped her complete the online application for the part-time job and put in a good word for her to the head librarian. The library opened at nine, which gave Minnie plenty of time to get ready, eat breakfast and catch the bus. She was thrilled when she got the job, but Helen was skeptical. She gave it a month, tops. Minnie, however, loved her new job and its access to so many sources of information— magazines, books, newspapers, videos and computers. Not to mention meeting new people. After her shift, Roberta helped her learn how to navigate the internet, opening the door to a world of instant information. Minnie soon realized, however, that with her meager paycheck it would take months before she saved enough money for a round-trip ticket to Columbia plus lodging once she arrived.

She was faced with a hard choice: ask Helen for money, which she swore she wouldn't do, or wait months to see Anna. There was another option, though. Use Helen's credit card. Minnie knew it was risky—and illegal. She'd noticed that the credit card bill came at the end of the month and by that time Minnie planned to be in Columbia happily reunited with Anna. Not only did Minnie decide it was worth the risk, but she believed that Helen owed her. If it weren't for Helen arranging a hasty adoption for Anna, Minnie wouldn't be in the position she was now, estranged from her only child. Yes, she decided, Helen owed her this and so much more.

~

Louis and I hit the ground running. I thought about taking the keys to Emma's car, but that would add grand theft auto to my list of problems.

I turned to Louis, "I hope you have some cash on you. I've got an idea. We need to get to my old neighborhood in Kennison."

We boarded a local bus and walked the remaining blocks to my neighborhood. Louis commented on the big houses, wide streets and manicured lawns. No wonder Marco was demanding $500 grand from Dad. It looked as if we were well-off. As we approached my house, tattered yellow crime scene tape flapped forlornly in the breeze. Weeds poked up from the once cared-for lawn. Old newspapers moldered on the front walk. There wasn't a squad car in sight.

"Good," I commented, "They've eased up on the surveillance for my dad." I walked toward the garage and peered into a side window. "My mother's car is still here." I entered what I thought was the garage door passcode with no results. "Give me your shirt," I said to Louis.

"What for?"

"You'll see. Just give it to me."

I was asking him for the shirt off his back. Reluctantly, Louis removed his shirt, revealing his flabby, white torso. I plastered the sweaty shirt against the window, picked up a rock and smashed the glass.

"How am I supposed to wear it now with glass all over it?"

"Don't worry," I said as I shook glass shards from the shirt. "When we get into the house, you'll have a whole new wardrobe."

I used my shoe to clear the remaining shards of glass from the window frame and gingerly climbed in. "Come on," I called Louis. "Look, Mother's keys are in the cupholder, where she always used to leave them."

The door from the garage into the house was unlocked. I braced myself and stepped into the kitchen. Instead of wrapping me in happy childhood memories the deserted house whispered of sadness and death. There was no happy ending there. I shook off my grief and turned to Louis.

"Do you want to see my room?"

"I guess." Louis's indecision got on my nerves, but hey, he was the one who offered to come with me, not Emma, and for that I was grateful.

Averting my eyes from the spot where Mother's outline was taped to the kitchen floor, I hurried up the stairs and peered into my room. My bed was exactly as Debare and I had left it after making love for the first time; disheveled and quickly abandoned when we heard the fatal gunshots. I could faintly smell Debare's father's citrus aftershave on my pillow and stuffed it into a gym bag along with some clothes and underwear, leaving room for shampoo, toothpaste, a brush and deodorant.

"Come on, you need clothes, too." I led Louis to my parents' room, the bed meticulously made. Nobody had slept in it since before the shooting—or after. I rifled through Dad's dresser drawers and selected a few T-shirts and cargo shorts. "Here, try these on. I'll wait for you downstairs."

My house didn't feel like home anymore. It silently spoke to me of violence and secrets. There wasn't anything I wanted to take with me outside of the necessities in the gym bag. The house was a mausoleum of death. I vowed never to return.

"How's it going up there?" I called up to Louis. *How long did it take to try on a T-shirt and a pair of shorts?* I was anxious to get the heck out of there. Finally, Louis appeared wearing one of Dad's shirts and his shorts. It was an improvement over our dirty, sweaty clothes, although Louis wasn't nearly as fit as my dad. The shirt stretched across his flabby belly.

I opened the garage door. Louis got in the driver's seat of Mother's car. The engine cranked a few times and caught. Louis revved it while I slammed into the passenger side.

"Where to?" he asked.

Good question.

~

Over the next few weeks Roberta taught Minnie how to log onto the computer and search for information on the Internet. When Minnie felt sufficiently confident in her computer skills, she decided to make her move. Before Helen got home from work one afternoon, Minnie went straight to her computer and turned it on. She didn't know Helen's password, but Roberta had mentioned that some people use a virtual keychain to store their passwords while others wrote them down and hid them. Frantically, Minnie began looking for a list. She looked under stacks of papers, in random books, on shelves. She ran her hand under the leather desk pad and pulled out a neatly typed list of usernames, passwords and credit card information. She was so relieved she nearly cried. She entered Helen's password and waited.

"Minnie, are you home?" Minnie quickly turned off the computer and slipped the list back under the desk pad.

Later, at dinner, Minnie asked Helen if she could use her computer to set up an email account. She tried to make it sound like it wasn't a big deal. She didn't let on that she'd already discovered her passwords.

"You've come a long way, Minnie. You got a job and now you're learning your way around the Internet. Of course, you can use my computer." For the first time Helen seemed genuinely pleased with Minnie's progress. Minnie did the dishes, hesitating before going up-stairs to Helen's office.

"I guess I'll need the password," she said nonchalantly, covering her tracks.

Minnie brought up the bus company website, selected the arrival and departure dates and times, then clicked *Next* to the payment sec-tion. Carefully, she added Helen's credit card number. She clicked *Next* again and held her breath. *Thank you for your order* appeared on the screen. *You will receive an email confirmation shortly.*

No worries, she'd just print the email when it arrived then delete it. Helen wouldn't be the wiser. Until, of course, the credit card bill came. Minnie planned to be with Anna by then. She was relieved that she'd bought the ticket, but she felt guilty, too. She'd stolen from He-len. She promised herself that she'd repay Helen for the ticket.

Now that she'd made the reservation, she couldn't just show up at Anna's house unannounced. She had two weeks to contact her and let her know that she was her birth mother and wanted to meet her. A telephone call was too risky. Anna might simply hang up when she discovered who it was. A letter. Minnie would write Anna a letter.

There was so much Minnie wanted to say to Anna, but she thought it best to tell her that she'd only recently found out that she wasn't dead as she had been told, and that she had never stopped loving or missing her. She would explain everything when they met face to face. She ended by saying that she hoped Anna would give her this chance. The next day she mailed the letter.

~

Louis and I didn't waste time or gas cruising around the neighborhood. Mother's army green car was easily recognizable by the neighbors. If they saw it on the street they'd wonder if it was stolen, maybe call the police. Best not to draw attention. I told Louis to take the interstate entrance ramp and blend in with traffic. But where to go? The homeless encampment and the hope of seeing Minnie hadn't released its hold on me.

"Take this exit," I directed at the last possible moment. Louis swerved and cut off a guy in a beat-up pickup truck who laid on the horn and made obscene gestures. The neighborhood around 1929 was the same, shabby and run-down as ever. Louis pulled into the gravel parking lot and killed the engine.

"What is this place?" he asked.

"This is where I used to come with my friend Natalie to visit Minnie, a homeless woman. It's the last place Marco would look for us. Not many people know it exists."

I fell silent, remembering the school field trip with Mr. Helm when I'd first met Minnie. Or when Emma drove Natalie and me so we could bring food and clothing for the homeless. Even Debare had come with me to help find Minnie after she disappeared.

"Hey! Earth to Mia." Louis nudged me, interrupting my daydream. "Are we crashing here or what? It looks ripe."

"We might have to. Mother kept a blanket in the trunk for emergencies. We can sleep in the car tonight."

The next morning, we awoke to the sound of footsteps crunching on gravel. I got out of the car, stretched my cramped legs and approached a young woman walking with an unruly toddler in tow.

"What's going on?" I asked.

"Today's the food pantry. We stock up on the perishables we can eat in a couple of days and all the staples we can carry." She hurried along, not wanting to lose her place in the queue.

"Hey Louis," I called. "C'mon. We're going to the food pantry."

"Why not just drive?" Louis asked, yawning and stretching.

"Because we're one of them, now. If we want to fit in...we walk. We're both technically homeless."

We collected our share of food: bread, peanut butter, jelly and then walked back to the encampment. "Remind me to bring a bag next time," I said. We stashed the food in the car, grabbed the blanket, removed the floor mats, and walked toward the viaduct to claim a spot to sleep. The only unoccupied spaces were deep within where it was permanently dark and dank.

"We'll have to watch for a place to open up nearer the entrance," I said.

"Oh, yeah?" Louis mused. "Is this going to be permanent?"

"Maybe. Do you have a better idea?"

After a couple of days, the novelty of being homeless wore off. I was bored and Louis slept a lot.

"I'm going to listen to the car radio," I said. As I approached, a guy was hanging around the car, intending to steal it. He looked scruffy, around sixty, but looks could be deceiving among the homeless, I knew.

"Hey, what's going on?" I demanded.

"Are you that girl? The one who used to come around looking for Minnie? I saw you and your boyfriend snooping around."

I eyed him suspiciously. "He's not my boyfriend and who wants to know?" I crossed my arms over my chest, trying to look imposing.

"If you are her, and I think you are, someone's been looking for *you* lately.

"Oh really? Who's looking for me—if I am that girl?"

The cat-and-mouse game continued until I blurted, "I get it. We both want something. I want to know who's looking for me. What do you want?"

"Give me that food in the car and drive me to the liquor store and I'll tell you."

Although I didn't have a driver's license, I felt confident enough to drive him to the local liquor store in return for finding out who had been looking for me.

"Get in," I said grudgingly. I drove him to a seedy 'packaged goods' store a short distance away and waited while he rambled in the door. After a few minutes he returned clutching a brown paper bag to his chest. I confronted him. "A deal's a deal. Who's looking for me?"

"A good-looking guy. Black. Well-dressed. Obviously not from around here."

I gasped and clasped my hands over my mouth. Soundlessly I mouthed his name. "Debare!"

~

Minnie began preparing for her bus trip. She packed her clothes in a suitcase she found in a closet and put toiletries in a plastic bag. She stocked up on snacks and checked out a couple of paperbacks for the long trip. Every day she made a point of being the first to the mailbox to look for a letter from Anna, but as the days slipped by with no response, she realized she had to decide. Should she continue with her plan or cancel the trip?

Minnie told her boss that she would be gone for a week due to family business, but to Roberta she opened up about her fears—that either Anna hadn't received her letter or if she had she was ignoring it. Who could be so heartless to ignore a plea from your estranged mother?

Minnie confided to Roberta that if she'd known that Anna had survived pneumonia as an infant, she would never have let her go.

With all the drama about Minnie's proposed reunion with her daughter, Roberta didn't mention the teenage girl who often came to the library searching through public records for someone. She came daily for weeks then suddenly stopped. Roberta thought for a few moments. She remembered that the girl was looking for a woman named Minnie! What were the odds? It seemed too much of a coincidence that Minnie might be the person she was looking for.

The bus to Columbia was scheduled to leave downtown Kennison at noon. Helen would be at work. Minnie would leave a note, she decided. She was nervous enough without risking a confrontation with Helen, who'd made it clear that she didn't approve of Minnie reaching out to Anna. Minnie was torn. She still hadn't heard from Anna. Should she scrap her plan and wait for a reply? Or should she go ahead, no matter what? That night as she lay in bed, she still hadn't made up her mind. *I'll know in the morning,* she thought.

Over morning coffee with Helen, Minnie tried acting like it was just another day.

"Any plans today?" Helen asked.

"The usual—the library then home. You?"

"Same thing—work then home."

After Helen left, Minnie made her decision. She called for a taxi. Her plan was in motion.

~

Debare was back from Nigeria! We had lost touch since the kidnapping. My phone was gone and I had no way to contact him. I hadn't forgotten about him, but so much had happened since he left for Nigeria. I'd moved in with Emma, seen Dad for the first time since Mother's murder, went to 1929 looking for Minnie, got kidnapped, escaped, got recaptured, and escaped again! Knowing that he was out there looking for me gave me hope. I wanted—needed—to be swept up into the safety and warmth of his embrace. I hurried to tell Louis the good news.

"Debare's back and he's been looking for me!" I gushed.

"Who the hell is Debare and why should I care?" Louis mumbled, half asleep.

"Debare's my boyfriend. He can get us out of this mess!"

"I didn't know you had a boyfriend. Where's he been?"

"In Nigeria, but he's back now and he can help us."

"Great. Wake me up when he gets here." True to form, Louis missed the point. I let him sleep and set out to find Debare.

I pulled up to Debare's house and parked Mother's army green car at the curb. There was a delivery truck in the driveway unloading groceries. Debare's mother was at the front door calling for Debare to help her bring the boxes and bags inside. I watched from the car. Debare wore jeans and a brightly colored African shirt that high-lighted his muscular arms and rich dark skin. He looked older than I remembered, more a man now than a boy. My pulse quickened. Every nerve ending crackled with anticipation at the sight of him. I bolted from the car, running across the lawn and calling his name. Debare dropped the box he was carrying and lifted me off my feet, hugging and kissing me while I wrapped my arms and legs around him and sobbed with happiness and relief. His mother smiled at the happy re-union.

"I tried calling you every day, but my calls always went straight to voice mail. Eventually, your mailbox was full. I wrote you letters that you won't receive for weeks. What happened to you?" Debare asked.

"I'll get the rest of these," Debare's mother said and didn't object when we charged upstairs and slammed to the door to Debare's room, eager for our private reunion.

To feel Debare in my arms brought tears and laughter, sometimes simultaneously. The frustration and fear the kidnapping melted away.

We wasted no time getting naked and made love, holding each other afterwards.

"I have so much to tell you," I said, "but now I really need a nap. I'm exhausted. I've been sleeping at *1929*...or trying to."

I closed my eyes. Debare gently covered me with the blanket. After I awoke from the much-needed nap I splashed cold water on my face and raked my fingers through my hair. I checked herself out in the mirror, frowned, and went downstairs. Debare was in the laundry room stuffing weeks of dirty laundry into the washer.

"You look like a man on a mission," I said, watching him from the hallway. "You're supposed to separate the darks from the whites, you know."

"Thanks for the tip, but I've got this," he smiled.

"Is your dad home? I need to talk to him about...my situation. I'm basically homeless." I was silent for a few moments. "Oh my God, I forgot to tell you about Louis."

"Did you find someone else while I was gone?" He looked hurt and betrayed.

"No! No way, Debare. I have so much to tell you. So much has happened since you've been gone. How was your trip, by the way?"

"Our family vacation to Nigeria really opened my eyes. Until you travel to another country, especially in Africa, you can't appreciate what we've got here: access to the Internet, cable TV, movies, concerts, shopping, food. You name it."

"We've got all those things, sure, but we've also a real problem with gun violence. I wouldn't be in the situation I am now—homeless and motherless—if it weren't for guns."

"Sorry. I haven't forgotten. I know you've been through hell with Natalie's death and then your mother's. It's a problem in other countries, too. Illegal firearms are rampant in Nigeria. They come from weapons dealers, many from the United States, I'm told." We were momentarily silent.

"Hop in the car, I want you to meet Louis, who saved my life—twice."

~

The taxi idled at the curb in front of Helen's house. With no response to her letter, Minnie had to decide. She closed the door behind her and walked the few steps to the waiting taxi.

"To the bus terminal, please." Her journey had begun. A new and exciting world with endless possibilities was unfolding before her.

She thought about the people who cared about her. Mia, the sweet high-school student who returned to the camp with offerings of food and clothing. Roberta, the librarian who befriended her and taught her how to use the computer. And then there was Helen who cared but for the wrong reasons; guilt and fear of being exposed. Still, if Helen hadn't searched for her and offered her a home she wouldn't be on the verge of a new life. For the first time that she could remember, Minnie looked toward the future with hope.

~

I got behind the wheel of Mother's car and started the engine.

"Did you get your license while I was gone?" Debare asked. I shook my head. "Then move over, I'm driving," I scooted over as he pulled away from the curb. "Besides, I want to hear about everything that happened."

I took a moment to gather my thoughts. "After you left for Nigeria, my father showed up at Emma's apartment where I was staying. I wasn't supposed to know, but I heard him talking to Emma and confronted him. He said he loved me and was making sure I was safe. After he left in a hurry, I demanded that Emma explain their relationship and what part she played in his business. I didn't know what or whom to believe."

The next morning, I went the homeless camp looking for Minnie and ended up getting kidnapped by Marco and his gang. We were holed up in a cornfield when I convinced Louis to escape with me. Debare listened intently, nodding his head, occasionally glancing in my direction and murmuring *wow* and *that's incredible.*

"Louis and I escaped to Emma's apartment and were recaptured when Marco followed the pizza guy in the door. And now I'm here with you." I snuggled next to him as he drove, touching his arm, making sure he was real.

"My God. You're lucky to be alive! I'm sorry I wasn't here for you." Debare said as we approached the 1929 parking lot.

It didn't take long to find Louis. He was in the same spot on his makeshift bed. Louis wasn't one to make big plans. He had decided that the safest place for him was with the homeless. He didn't mind sleeping on the ground, wearing the same clothes day after day, and scrounging for food. He embraced the homeless life.

"Louis, get up," I said, nudging him with my toe. "I want you to meet someone."

Louis peered out from under the blanket. His red curly hair looked like a clown's wig. He propped himself up on his elbows. "This is my boyfriend, Debare, the guy I've been telling you about."

"Hi." Louis reached out to shake Debare's hand. "Your girlfriend, she's something else. She's the reason I'm here. I mean that in the best possible way. Otherwise, we'd both be..."

"I know. She told me everything on the way over here. Thanks for keeping her safe."

"Louis, why don't you come with us? You could stay at my parents' empty house, at least for a while, 'til things cool down."

"Thanks, but no thanks. I'm not staying where someone got murdered. No offense. Plus, that's the first place Marco will come looking if he hasn't already. I'm just going to lay low for a while until things cool down."

"OK, then. Thanks for helping me escape—twice. Stay safe." We turned to leave. Louis pulled the blanket back up over his head.

"He doesn't look like a dangerous criminal," Debare said as we walked back to the car.

"He's not. He got mixed up with Marco because he needed money and Marco promised him no one would get hurt. Marco, of course, is a liar and a murderer."

When we arrived at Debare's house the groceries were put away and his mother was in the kitchen preparing a spicy vegetarian stew, one of Debare's favorite dishes from his homeland.

"Mrs. A, I'm so grateful for everything you've done for me. I was staying with my best friend's sister while you were gone, but then everything went south in a hurry." I began.

"When we returned, we saw your photo on TV and that of your father. We were all very concerned for you. What happened?" Debare's mother asked.

"It's a long story," I began, "but, yes, I was kidnapped, twice in fact, and the kidnappers are still at large. I found out that my father, who is also at large, is an international gun runner, dealing in every sort of weapon imaginable to countries where it's against the law to own guns." I stifled a yawn and rubbed my eyes. "I'm sorry, I don't mean to be rude, but retelling the whole nightmare is exhausting."

Mrs. A came over and put her arms around me, hugging me gently. "I understand. Enough for one day. Should I make up the guest bedroom for you, Mia?" She said with a sweet smile that spoke of a mother's concern. Debare was so lucky to have her as his mother.

"I would love that," I replied, a little choked up, so grateful that I had a safety net, a place to call home amid my chaotic life.

"Will Mr. Adebayo be home later? I'd like to talk to him if he has time." I asked.

"Of course. He went to the office today, but he'll be home for dinner. He'll be happy to talk to you." Debare's mother was striking with plaited hair swept away from her face revealing her flawless toffee complexion and high cheekbones.

~

Minnie slept fitfully during the bus ride sometimes feigning sleep to avoid the woman sitting next to her who talked incessantly about her grandchildren and insisted on showing photos. Minnie pondered the possibility of having a grandchild of her own. She pictured a sweet, towheaded girl running toward her shouting, 'Grandma!' Best not to get her hopes up, she decided. Helen never mentioned grandchildren, but she was not a reliable source of information. What mattered now was meeting Anna. A grandchild would be icing on the cake, more than she dared hope for.

She caught a glimpse of the capitol dome from the window as the traffic slowed. Her breath caught in her throat and her heart fluttered like a netful of butterflies. Am I having a heart attack? Please, God, not now. Minnie closed her eyes and took a few deep breaths that calmed her and slowed her heart rate. She had come too far to have her dreams dashed by a heart attack.

As her destination approached, she began to question everything. What if she didn't measure up to Anna's standards? Anna was an educated, professional woman. Minnie had nothing to offer but the fact that she had given birth to her.

Another disturbing thought entered Minnie's mind. What if Anna thought that Minnie's reason for reaching out to her was money and a place to live? Nothing could be further from the truth, but Anna only knew what her adoptive parents and Helen had told her. Minnie's letter made it clear that she wanted to set the record straight and wasn't asking for anything in return, except a place in Anna's heart. But had Anna received it? Not knowing Anna's response was an added worry.

Travelers with backpacks clutching shopping bags and carefully wrapped parcels milled about the bus station. Minnie hailed a taxi and handed the driver a scrap of paper with Anna's address. He peered at

Minnie through the rearview mirror and merged into traffic without saying a word. They bypassed the city center and continued until the scenery was green and lush with manicured lawns and shrubbery. The suburb of Monroe was dotted with stately mansions, some with plaques indicating historical landmarks. Minnie felt like she was going back in time to another era. The streets were quiet and shaded, overhung by an archway of trees. The driver slowed down in front of an imposing two-story Colonial-style home set back from the street. An ornate iron gate guarded the driveway leading to the house.

"Hello? I'm Minnie Anderson here to see Anna Phillips." Minnie said into the speaker mounted on a post. Nothing happened. After a few anxious moments the gate began to slowly open allowing the taxi to proceed up the circular drive to the front steps. The driver deposited Minnie's suitcase on the bottom step, she paid him and he drove down the driveway. Minnie stared after him, wishing she'd asked him to wait. She stared at the imposing oak door and knocked twice with the burnished metal ring hanging from a lion's mouth.

~

It was well after seven when Debare's father returned from work. I liked that his family ate dinner together, even though he worked long hours. While we waited, Debare told me that his family's yearly trip to Nigeria was marked with celebrations—feasting and bonfires honoring his parents and the successful future the elders predicted for him.

"I wore a kufi, a traditional men's cap, and a matching agbada, a sort of flowing kaftan, to the celebrations. It's not all for show, though. I have the responsibility of carrying on family traditions in America. All the aunties wanted to feed me their special dishes and asked if I had a girlfriend in America. When I told them about you, Mia, they hugged and kissed me, saying it was a good match."

When everyone was seated at the table, Mrs. Adebayo spooned generous portions of stew into large ceramic bowls accompanied by crusty bread. The stew was delicious, seasoned with exotic spices that

I had never tasted. I owed this family so much for taking her into their home and making me feel welcome after my life was once again turned upside down. It was a refuge that I wished I would never have to leave.

After dinner Mrs. A mentioned to her husband that I wanted to speak with him. He brought his coffee mug into the study and invited me to sit on the soft leather sofa. Debare hung back, unsure of his place in the conversation.

"Anything I say to your father I can say to you," I assured him.

Instead of sitting behind his stately desk, Mr. A pulled up a chair near the sofa.

"My father is in a lot of trouble. I've seen on TV that he's a dangerous criminal wanted on suspicion of murder. I…I still can't believe he killed my mother." I said, perched nervously on the edge of the sofa.

Mr. A listened, measuring his words before speaking. "Mia, your father is not who you think he is. He's been leading a double life. We've been tracking him for a couple of years."

I was confused. "We? Who's 'we'?"

"I work for IBEAT, the International Bureau for the Eradication of Arms Trafficking. I was assigned to track your father and his business dealings. That's why we moved here. I'm sorry to have to tell you this, Mia, but your father illegally sells weapons of all kinds internationally. It doesn't matter whether they are friends or enemies of our country. He started out selling handguns and assault weapons on a small scale. He branched out to military armaments. He was approached by rivals in the business to consolidate and share his business contacts. He refused."

"Did you know about this, Debare?" Tears rolled down my cheeks. "Please tell me you didn't."

"Mia, I swear to you I knew nothing about it. My father doesn't share information about his work. But you're directly involved. He didn't know we were dating until a short time ago." He squeezed my hand while I rested my head on his shoulder. We sat silently for a moment while I let his father's words sink in.

"We're pretty sure we know who is responsible for your mother's murder." Mr. A said.

"I'm pretty sure I know, too." I said. "It's Marco, the guy who kidnapped me."

"The Bureau has enough information to indict Marco on weapons and money laundering charges. Add kidnapping and murder to that and Marco should be going away for a very long time. We're waiting to make the arrest because we want to include everyone in his circle. You can help us, Mia. Tell me what happened."

I closed my eyes. I felt old and tired. What happened to proms, sleepovers with girlfriends, doing each other's hair and make-up? I was plunged head-first into deceit, murder and kidnapping. I could never go back to the naïve freshman who agreed to steal guns for what I thought was a good cause. That girl didn't exist anymore. I swallowed the rage that smoldered inside and could explode at any time. But not today.

"What do you want to know? I'll tell you everything." Two hours later, exhausted from retelling my story, I said goodnight to Mr. A and trudged upstairs to bed. Debare and I kissed good night outside his bedroom door and retreated to our separate rooms.

~

Minnie didn't know how long she had been waiting on the porch. She felt suddenly lightheaded and abruptly sat down on the granite steps. "Are you alright?" A woman's voice startled Minnie from her trance. The woman, too old to be Anna, helped her to her feet.

"Can I get you a glass of water?" The woman asked.

"Yes, please." Minnie said, still feeling unsteady on her feet. Judging by the woman's expensive clothes, jewelry and stylish hair, she clearly wasn't a housekeeper. She returned momentarily with a bottle of mineral water.

"You are Minnie Anderson?" It was more a statement than a question.

"Yes, I'm Minnie. I wrote Anna to say I was coming."

"Anna showed me your letter. Apparently, you didn't receive her response. She's at work now. She planned to meet you at the Sunrise Café tomorrow at 1pm. Please, come inside. Can I call you a taxi? I don't know what your plans are, but there's a motel in town, down the street from the café." The woman remarked.

Minnie was overwhelmed by the grandeur of the foyer. The high ceilings, elaborate staircase and marble floor made her feel like she should speak in hushed tones.

"Yes, I made a reservation there. Thank you."

An awkward silence separated the two women as each scanned the other without appearing too obvious. Minnie thought to explain her visit to the woman who had yet to introduce herself but thought better of it. Anna was the person she had come to see.

Minnie spent the evening sitting by the motel pool watching the daylight fade from pink to purple. Insects whirred around the pool lights. She retreated to her room and turned on the TV for company. She picked up the desk phone and dialed an outside line.

"Helen? It's Minnie. I wanted to let you know I'm safe."

"Thank God! I was worried. Where are you?"

"I'm in the capitol, Columbia." No one spoke for a long moment.

"I read your note. Have you met with Anna?"

"Not yet. We're meeting tomorrow at a coffee shop."

"I hope it goes well for you, that meeting Anna is everything you hoped it would be."

"Thanks, I'll let you know." Minnie paused then added, "Helen, there's something I have to tell you. I used your credit card to pay for my bus fare."

"Minnie, I would have given you the money if you'd just asked me."

"I'm sorry. I'll pay you back, every penny."

"The credit card bill came and I saw the charge. Thank you for telling me yourself."

"Well, goodnight, Helen. I'll be in touch."

Sleep was impossible. So many thoughts raced through Minnie's head. What to say, what to wear? Should she apologize? For what? It wasn't her fault. She slept fitfully and awoke as the sky brightened. She felt like she hadn't slept at all. After a warm shower she relaxed. She decided to walk down to the café for coffee and a light breakfast. Seeing the place where she was to meet Anna might help put her mind at ease.

As the meeting time approached Minnie put on her blue polyester travel dress, purchased specifically for the occasion and stood in front of the bathroom mirror. Too dressy for the café, she thought. She changed into slacks and a blouse. Not dressy enough and changed back into the dress. She added a yellow scarf before heading out the door, hopeful that the meeting would go well, nervous that it wouldn't,

Minnie arrived early and sat near a window. She had been waiting about twenty minutes when a tall slender woman with white blonde hair, shoulders back, head held high, walked regally down the sidewalk and entered the café. She stopped at the counter and ordered a coffee. Coffee in hand, she turned and scanned the patrons. She wore linen slacks that accentuated her long legs, a silk blouse open at the neck, and beige leather flats.

Minnie stood and took one halting step.

"Anna?" She was trembling. This was it. The moment she had been dreaming about. As her beautiful daughter walked toward her, it felt surreal, like a dream.

Anna nodded. Minnie indicated the seat across from her.

"You must be Minnie," Anna said in a low, throaty voice.

"I am."

"I hardly know what to say. Your letter was a shock." Anna sat and stared across the table at Minnie. "It hardly gave me time to prepare…emotionally."

"I'm sorry it was short notice, but you have haunted me my entire life. We thought you were dead—your father and me."

"Why now, after all these years?"

"When I learned, only recently, that you were alive, it became my mission to find you and here I am."

They sat silently, Minnie rearranging her scarf, Anna starring off into the distance, her hands folded neatly on the table. Finally, Minnie broke the silence.

"Who answered your door yesterday? She was very kind to me."

"My mother." She hesitated for effect. "The only mother I've ever known."

"I'm so sorry, Anna. You were taken from me. I didn't have a chance to be your mother. I spent my life thinking you were dead. Imagine how I felt when I found out you were alive."

"How did you find out?" Anna eyed Minnie suspiciously.

"The woman who arranged your adoption tracked me down and told me the truth, finally, after a lifetime of deceit." Tears welled up in Minnie's eyes, but she managed to keep it together. This may be her only chance to talk to Anna and she needed to tell her side of the story.

"Why would she do that?" Anna said after hearing the story. "Did someone pay her off? I'm an attorney. I could find out."

"She may have been. I don't know. She admitted to placing you with a couple she felt would take better care of you than your father and me. But that doesn't change the fact that what she did was wrong. It ruined my life. Your father left and I had to live on the street."

"Is that why you're here? For money? A place to live?" Anna's brow wrinkled above fierce green eyes.

"Like I said in my letter, I don't want anything from you. Only a chance to meet you and get to know you." Minnie reached out to Anna's slender hand across the table. Anna reflexively pulled hers away.

Glancing at her watch, Anna rose to leave, "It's late and I've got afternoon appointments."

"Please, you can't just cut me off. I've come a long way. Please." Hot tears flowed down Minnie's cheeks. "I'm your mother."

"How long are you in town?" Anna asked, as if setting up a business meeting.

"I'm not on a timetable. Please, Anna. I'm at the motel, room 28."

"I'll be in touch." With that Anna sailed out the door with the aplomb of a movie star.

Minnie was stunned at Anna's coldness, treating her like a client you might meet over coffee. She hadn't expected miracles, but nothing like this. If only she could penetrate Anna's defensive armor. But how? She didn't have anything in common with her daughter except her genes. Anna's world was as alien to Minnie as Minnie's was to Anna. Was Anna capable of letting her guard down and taking that first step, that first difficult step? Anna was educated and glamorous. Minnie was common, the type of person you would pass on the street without a second glance. Surely Anna had compassion and forgiveness deep inside. Minnie was determined to find it.

The next day Minnie again ate breakfast at the café then ambled down Main Street with its trendy boutiques and organic grocery store. She found herself at the library, a safe and familiar place. While scanning local newspapers and happened upon an article about Anna's contribution to a local homeless shelter. Minnie shook her head. How ironic, she thought, that Anna publicly helped strangers, but was unwilling to acknowledge her own mother's fate.

On her walk back to the motel, Minnie passed a storefront with red, purple and orange jars of homemade jams and jellies in the window. The jars shone like gems in the sunlight. Fascinated, Minnie stopped and purchased jars of grape and strawberry preserves. She nestled the jars in the bottom of her purse and continued to the hotel. She spent the rest of the day watching television and reading a mystery novel she had purchased at the library's used bookstore. I'll give it another day for Anna to reach out. After all, her resources were limited. She'd done all she could. It was up to Anna, now.

~

That night, Minnie awoke from a dream that seemed so real it was like watching a movie. Two women were sitting at a kitchen table drinking coffee and a little girl, around four years old, burst into the room crying and clutching a stuffed animal. "What's wrong?" cried both women.

"My puppy's tail came off!" She held out the tail.

"Don't worry, I can fix it," said one of the women as she went to get her sewing kit. The other woman scooped the child into her arms and consoled her. The dream left Minnie with such a peaceful, loving feeling that it brought tears to her eyes. *It's only a dream*, she told herself, but she tucked the image away. *Things that are broken can be repaired.*

Another day waiting for Anna's call loomed. Minnie grabbed her purse and headed outside into the cool morning breeze. She just walked, with no destination in mind. She found herself in Anna's exclusive neighborhood. Funny, she thought, passersby might mistake her for a domestic, but it didn't bother her. Cleaning houses was honest work, nothing to be ashamed of.

The gate to Anna's estate was open so Minnie walked purposely up the long driveway, up the granite stairs, knocked and waited. The door slowly opened. It was the woman who had previously answered the door, Anna's mother.

"Good morning," Minnie said.

"Good morning. I'm sorry, but Anna isn't home," the woman said apologetically.

"I didn't come for Anna. You were so kind to me the other day that I brought you something." Minnie rummaged in her purse, pulled out the jars of jam and handed them to Anna's adoptive mother.

"I'm Minnie, by the way."

"I'm Victoria," she hesitated. "Anna's mother." She eyed the gem-colored jars appreciatively. "Thank you for these."

"You're welcome," Minnie said. "I'm Anna's mother, too, her birth mother."

Seconds ticked by as the two women stood assessing each other in the morning sunlight.

"Yes, Anna told me that you had reached out to her. Where are my manners?" Victoria said. "Please, come inside."

She led Minnie through the magnificent entranceway, past the breathtaking staircase to a modern kitchen with evidence that people lived in this sterile mansion.

A half-full mug of coffee cooled on the table.

"I was just having my morning coffee. Can I offer you some?" Victoria asked.

"I'd love a cup," Minnie replied.

"How about some toast? We can taste this lovely jam," she said, eyeing the sparkling jars.

Victoria got a far-away look. "When Anna was little, we had a summer cottage with a grape arbor. Wild strawberries grew in the meadow. We made jam together. I took it as a good omen when you showed up at the door with these." She held the jars in the light.

Minnie whispered, "I would have loved to have made jam with Anna. But I'm glad she got the chance to do those things with you."

The women sipped coffee and nibbled on toast and jam. After a while Victoria said, "I can't imagine what you've been through. You've been denied all the joys and sorrows of motherhood. But my husband and I were told that you had abandoned Anna. If only we'd known the truth."

"When I see the beautiful, successful woman Anna has become I know I could never have offered her all the opportunities that you were able to. Still, she would be beautiful no matter what and success-ful as well if Jim and I had raised her. I'll never know."

Then Victoria did something unexpected. She reached across the table and placed her hand over Anna's. "We're both her mother. You gave birth to her and I had the good fortune to raise her." Minnie smiled and grasped Victoria's hand, grateful that she had opened her heart. If only Anna would do the same. Before Minnie left Victoria invited her to dinner the following evening.

"Are you sure?" Minnie asked. "Anna might not approve."

"Don't worry about Anna. Leave that to me." Victoria said.

"Thank you. That's very kind. Can I bring something?"

"Just bring yourself. That will be more than enough."

~

While Minnie was grateful to Victoria for the opportunity to sit down and share a meal with her daughter, she was nervous. Everything she felt lacking about herself—social graces, education, culture, wardrobe, and so much more loomed over her that night as she lay in bed imagining dinner at the mansion. Sleep was again elusive, so she sat outside watching people walk their dogs, couples out for an evening walk and cars driving down Main Street.

Eventually she went inside for a few hours of restless sleep. During the day she walked downtown and peered into shop windows, selecting the outfit she would wear to dinner that night if she had the money. As the time approached to dress for dinner, she selected black slacks with a pale blue blouse. She styled her hair as the stylist at the salon had shown her. She called a taxi and took one last look in the mirror before heading out.

Victoria greeted her at the door and led her into the living room where she had put out a charcuterie tray and offered Minnie a glass of white wine. They chatted about the weather but the elephant in the room was, *where is Anna?*

"Anna phoned and said she's running late at the office." Victoria said.

Anna's work obviously came first. Did she even know that Victoria had invited Minnie to dinner? Victoria couldn't have been more gracious, keeping the conversation going and trying to make Minnie feel welcome in the elegant house. Victoria glanced at her watch, "We should go in, Marta hates it when dinner is delayed."

The dining room table was set for three with delicate porcelain dinnerware and gold-rimmed goblets with stems so slender that Minnie was afraid they might break. Just as the two women sat down opposite each other, Anna swept into the room and sat at the head of the table.

"Minnie has graciously agreed to join us for dinner tonight seeing as though you've been too busy to meet with her. She's leaving tomorrow and I thought..." Victoria began and somehow managed not to make it sound like she was chastising her daughter.

Anna addressed the seated women. "Sorry I'm late. I'm on the board of the new homeless shelter in the city, a state-of-the-art facility with classrooms, private rooms for the residents, access to medical care and so much more. We're very proud of our accomplishment."

Minnie froze, her delicate wine glass suspended in midair. Was Anna deliberately being cruel or was she so wrapped up in herself that she didn't know or care how her announcement affected her and her own history of homelessness? Was she trying to humiliate her or did she simply not care?

"Anna!" Victoria gasped. "Minnie, I'm so sorry. Our Anna has forgotten her manners."

Anna's face became distorted with rage. "First of all, what do you mean by *our* Anna?

Besides our biology, I reject any connection to *that* woman. And no, I haven't forgotten my manners, but maybe you have, Mother, by inviting her into *my* house, without *my* permission."

Minnie was stunned. She had never knowingly hurt anyone in her life. How could her own flesh and blood treat her so cruelly?

Victoria put her fork down, Minnie her wine glass. The women looked down at their untouched dinner, speechless. Finally, Minnie gathered the courage to speak.

"Anna, we could use your expertise in Kennison." Minnie said softly, searching her daughter's eyes for a glimmer of compassion.

"Every community has a homeless problem," Anna said with authority.

"We're people, not problems," Minnie replied, which ended the conversation.

The meal continued in uncomfortable silence except for Minnie's compliments about the fish. Minnie conducted herself with dignity. She left immediately after dinner, refusing coffee and dessert in the living room. Her attempt to remain stoic was rapidly deteriorating. She wanted to return to the hotel as soon as possible, have a good cry, then pack her bag and return to Kennison. What waited for her there, she wasn't sure, but she suspected that Helen would be self-righteous and smug without saying the words, *I told you so.*

~

Hazy days and chilly evenings signaled the end of Summer. I was due back at school. My 'how I spent my summer vacation' essay would be quite a blockbuster, I mused. *I witnessed a brutal murder, was kidnapped, escaped, was recaptured and escaped again.* Fact is indeed stranger than fiction, I thought. I hoped I could fly under the radar for as long as possible. I didn't want to be the center of attention at Jane Addams. I wanted to be invisible and finish my senior year with as little drama as possible.

There was one thing I needed to do during my last few days of freedom. Go to *1929* and check on Louis. I owed him that much. I'd bring him supplies, just like I'd done with Minnie. With all the bizarre twists and turns in my life, I still hadn't been able to reconnect with her. A trip to 1929 would offer some clues. I took a jar of peanut butter, a loaf of bread and a bag of cookies from the pantry and left a note that the food was for the homeless. I was certain that the Adebayo's wouldn't mind. I put them in Mothers' car. I had finally gotten my license after Debare took me driving and quizzed me on the written test.

The sky was brilliantly blue. Lacy orange and red maples heralded the arrival of Autumn. My footsteps crunched fallen leaves as I exited the car. It was quiet in 1929 as it usually was on a weekday morning. When you're homeless you don't set an alarm to get up for work or make your morning coffee. It wasn't hard to find Louis. His curly red hair sticking out from under a blanket gave him away. I gently prodded him.

"Wake up, sleepy head. I brought you some stuff."

Louis slowly opened his eyes and sat up when he saw it was me.

"Hey! What's up? I didn't expect you," Louis said.

"I couldn't just abandon you, could I? After everything we've been through together?"

"I guess not. How are you? Where are you living?"

I told him I was living at Debare's house, and I hadn't talked to Emma since we went over the balcony at her apartment.

On the way to the car, I stopped in my tracks. Standing outside the viaduct, her profile backlit in sunlight, was the woman who evoked memories of warmth and love. She was talking to a homeless man but didn't look homeless herself. Her clothes appeared new, her hair was neatly styled. Her shoes weren't from a thrift store. I approached and stood outside the woman's view. Aware of a presence, the woman turned and momentarily hesitated. Her face lit up with a broad smile, revealing white, even teeth.

"Mia! My guardian angel. I can't believe it. I thought I'd never see you again," she exclaimed, embracing me.

"Minnie! Is it really you? I've been searching for you, but so much got in my way."

"Same here," Minnie said, smiling.

We laughed, hugged, cried then laughed some more. Finally, I said, "Let's go somewhere where we can talk." We spent the rest of the afternoon at a café drinking tea and eating croissants with jam, catching up with each other's lives. Minnie explained how Helen had found her and took her into her home. She finally met her daughter, Anna, who had *not* died at birth (that was a story for another time, she said) but their reunion was a disaster. She didn't go into detail, but the sadness in her eyes said it all. She was visiting the camp today to reconnect with homeless friends and let them know she was okay. I shared the condensed version of my mother's violent murder, my father's disappearance and finally, my kidnapping and escape.

"I know, it seems unbelievable, a nightmare. I'm staying at my boyfriend's house. His parents said I could stay with them for as long as I wanted. I could never go back to the house where my mother was murdered. I'm basically homeless, like you. I'm here to check on Louis."

"Who's Louis?"

"He was one of my kidnappers." I laughed, shaking my head.

"Why in God's name would you care about him?" Minnie's brow furrowed with concern.

"He was supposed guard me, but he ended up helping me escape. Now he's hiding from Marco, the ringleader and the guy responsible for my mother's death."

Minnie gazed off into the distance. "It's a lot to take in, but I believe you, of course. It's like *my* story, unbelievable, but true."

Before they parted, Mia to Debare's and Minnie to Helen's, they agreed not to lose touch with each other again. They promised to meet for tea and pastries every week and if one of them didn't show up, the other would call to find out why. *That's what friends do, right?*

～

Marco returned to Emma's apartment to find Mia and Louis gone. Emma blamed it on AJ's incompetence.

"He was hanging in the hall smoking and listening to his headphones. I called for help, but he didn't hear me. It was two against one, I couldn't stop them."

"Stupid bitch, you should've tried harder!" Marco roared. "If I didn't need you to get to Dick Compton, I'd off you right now!" He pointed his gun at her from across the room. Emma sat silently on the sofa, where she had watched Mia and Louis bolt over the balcony.

"Don't think I won't do it!" He stormed into the kitchen and cracked open a can of beer.

Previous attempts for the money drop from Dick to Marco had failed. At the latest attempt Marco had a feeling that he was being followed and called it off at the last minute. It left Dick wondering if Marco only wanted the money or was setting him up for assassination.

Without her phone, Emma had no way to contact Dick and tell him that Mia had escaped—again. Everyone's survival depended on a successful money drop—Emma's, Dick's and Mia's.

"Tomorrow is his last chance to deliver, or everyone dies." Marco glanced from Emma to AJ, his eyes cold as steel on a winter's day. He took Emma's phone from his pocket and clicked on Dick's number.

"Here, talk to your boyfriend. Tell him it's now or never, and I do mean never, for everyone, you included."

Emma took the phone, her palms sweating.

"Dick, it's me." Her voice cracked and wavered while she explained the plan. "This is it, Dick. Your last chance to make it right. If you don't deliver the money Marco says we're all dead and that means me, too. You know he'll do it."

"Let me talk to Mia."

Before Emma could explain that Mia was gone, Marco grabbed the phone. "Tomorrow. Noon. At the chicken shack just off the highway, exit 53. You know the place." Marco ended the call and put the phone back in his pocket.

"We're on for tomorrow. If he doesn't show up, you're dead. Count on it."

Emma lay in bed terrified of what was sure to happen if Dick didn't deliver the cash. She tried counting backwards from one thousand, meditating, even doing yoga poses in the cramped space of the tiny bedroom, but nothing worked. *It's going to be a long night.*

The sound of the television blaring the morning news forced her out of bed and into the kitchen for coffee. *This may be my last cup of coffee, my last morning on this earth.*

She stood sipping her coffee while Marco sat on the sofa glued to the TV. By now Nina Compton's murder and Dick and Mia's disappearance were old news and had dropped from the headlines, but occasionally a television station flashed photos of Dick and Mia with a phone number asking for information. Marco turned the television off, satisfied that Dick was still at large and the transfer would happen.

Emma took a shower, savoring the warmth cascading over her head and down her body. She put on fresh jeans and a sweater. May as well dress for her last day. Waiting for noon was nerve-wracking. She sat on the bed reading a cheesy romance novel that she found in the closet. Anything to distract her from being hostage in this cramped apartment with a murderous sociopath and his clueless accomplice, AJ. Her senses were hyper-alert to the smell and taste of strong black coffee, the sound of the TV, the feel of her cozy sweater and the disgusting sight of Marco clipping his toenails on the sofa. *If I survive, I'm tossing that sofa.* Suddenly Marco barked that it was time to go. She sprang to attention.

"This is it. And don't even think about running. Get in the van, dammit!"

The odor of fried food hung in the air as Marco's van pulled into the parking lot of the chicken shack. He backed into a space, for a quick exit, Emma assumed. She was hemmed in between Marco and AJ on the front seat. More waiting. Marco opened the windows, but the stench outside was as bad as inside; cigarette smoke, discarded fast food wrappers, unwashed male bodies.

A dark blue sedan with tinted windows pulled slowly into the lot and parked nearby. The door opened and out stepped Dick Compton, looking like one of the homeless men from *1929*. He carried an over-stuffed duffel bag and tossed it on the ground.

"You two stay here." Marco barked. He bolted out of the van and slammed the door.

"Marco stood about ten feet from Dick, one hand in his jacket pocket. Dick held his hands palms up without being told.

"It's all there," Dick said, without taking his eyes off Marco.

Marco showed Dick his gun then stuffed it in his waistband while he bent down to unzip the bag.

Out of nowhere, a swarm of shiny black SUVs sped into the parking lot, blocking the exit and surrounding the van and sedan. A team of armed police slammed from the vehicles, pointing their weapons at Marco, demanding, "Toss your weapon and lay face down on the pavement."

Marco was momentarily frozen in place. He glanced at Dick and then did as he was told, assuming the position.

The uniformed officers were over him in seconds, handcuffing him and hoisting him to his feet. An officer read him his rights along with a laundry list of crimes for which he was being arrested, including, murder, racketeering, kidnapping, illegal weapons sales, and money laundering. Marco was led off to one of the SUVs which quickly sped away escorted by other official vehicles.

Emma and AJ remained in the van, uncertain what to do. An armed agent approached and barked, "Come out with your hands in the air." AJ was immediately handcuffed and led away.

Dick walked towards Emma and stopped. Emma closed the distance between them and buried her face in Dick's chest, crying softly.

"It's over," Dick said again and again. "Don't cry, Em, it's over. Everyone's safe now—you, me, and Mia."

The SUV with AJ sped away, sirens blaring, lights flashing. A black sedan pulled up. A tall, fit man with cropped hair, stepped out of the car. He surveyed the scene through dark aviator glasses then walked toward Emma and Dick.

"We did it. With your help we got Marco. He'll be incarcerated for a very long time," Mr. Adebayo said.

~

As was often the case, Debare's father was late to dinner that night. Mr. Adebayo walked in the door followed by Emma, Dad and a police officer. I stood speechless with no idea what was happening. Seeing Emma and my father, a cascade of emotions swept over me—love, anger, suspicion—and jealousy.

Debare stood next to me, supporting me. I stared at my father and Emma across the room. Debare's father was the first to speak. "Mia, before you judge your father, now that you know about his illegal weapons business, let me say that with his help—and Emma's, this afternoon the Bureau arrested Marco and AJ. We shut down the largest international weapons trafficking scheme uncovered to date. Other arrests will follow in the days ahead."

"But he's as guilty as the rest of them!" I blurted, pointing to my father.

"He'll have to answer for that. After your mother's death he agreed to cooperate with the authorities in exchange for leniency. Emma knew of his illegal business but didn't play an active role. She did help keep you safe, though. So here we are. Take advantage of this brief time with your father. If there's something you want to say, say it now. He'll be incarcerated tonight."

I stood frozen in place, trying to process this new information. I knew for certain that Dad hadn't killed Mother. He didn't pull the trigger, but his illegal activity—and greed was responsible. I had so many questions, like what part, if any, Emma played in my second escape, but no time to sort it all out. Dad took a step toward me. I flinched, turning away from him and into Debare.

"I...I don't know what or who to believe. My life has been a lie," I said to my father. "When I was a little girl, I wondered what you did for a living. Kids at school had fathers who were engineers, doctors, lawyers, everything under the sun, but I never knew what you did. If someone asked, I said that you stayed home and worked on your computer all day. After Mother's death I didn't know if you were dead or kidnapped. You weren't either, you were hiding. Because of you I could have died. I can't just forget everything that's happened."

"I am sorry, Mia. For all the pain I've caused. After Nina's death I knew it all had to end. I knew the next target would be you, that's part of the reason why I agreed to cooperate with the Bureau. That and to avenge your mother's death."

I was silent for a few moments. "What about you and Emma?"

He clutched Emma's hand. "I know it will take time, but I hope you'll accept Emma as your stepmother," Dick said.

"We're getting married," Emma said, smiling at Dick and squeezing his hand. He placed his other hand over Emma's belly. "You're going to be a big sister!"

I grimaced, feeling heat rising in my cheeks. "Am I supposed to be happy? Is that what you think? Because I'm not. I don't want to hear this—not now—not ever." I grabbed Debare's arm and stormed out of the room. I didn't see my father being led away in handcuffs.

Part IV

4

The following week Minnie and I met at the café as planned. I wanted to tell her about Emma's pregnancy and Dad's arrest. It weighed heavy on my mind and who better to tell than my surrogate mother, Minnie? We ordered and sat at what would become our usual table. I was quiet and Minnie picked up on it immediately.

"Do you want to talk about it?" She asked.

"My kidnappers, Marco and AJ, got arrested and I got to see my father for a few minutes before he went to jail, but..." I looked down at the croissant on my plate.

"But what? You know you can tell me anything."

"I thought that the worst was over now that I'm safe."

"But...?"

"They're getting married!" I blurted.

"Who's getting married? I'm confused."

"Emma and my father. They've been a couple all along."

"She's not much older than you. Am I right?" Minnie said cautiously.

"That's not the worst of it. They're having a baby. Ugh! It's so gross."

"You've been through so much, Mia." Minnie reached across the table and squeezed my hand. "Whatever happens with your father and his girlfriend is out of your control. It may take a long time for you to deal with your feelings. *Your* life is what's important now. Finishing school, dating, doing what girls your age do."

"I know, but my life will never be normal. I lost my best friend and my mother—and I have a felon for a father. I don't see how that can ever be normal. No way."

"Give it time, Mia. It may not seem like it now, but your life is full of possibilities. And you know I'll always be here if you need someone to talk to. Not that I have all the answers, but I can listen, and sometimes that's better than anything."

"I wish you were my mother." I sighed. "I feel so guilty, sometimes, that I wasn't closer to her before she died. We both put up walls and wouldn't let the other one in. If I'd known that she'd be suddenly taken from me, I would have been nicer, let her get closer. But it's too late now." My voice trailed off to a whisper.

"I never got over the loss of my Anna. A mother never gets over the loss of a child. Now that I've found her, though, the happy reunion I hoped for didn't happen. She refuses to accept me or let me into her life. What is it about girls and their mothers? It's so complicated! It's an important bond, but so easily splintered."

"I have an idea," I said, feeling hopeful for the first time in a while, "we can do the next best thing. You can be my surrogate mother and I'll be your stand-in daughter. We'll be the person each of us needs and wants but never had."

"I'd love that," Minnie said quietly as tears filled her eyes. We continued to sip our tea and munch on croissants and sweet rolls until it was time to leave.

"Until next week," I said as we embraced.

"Until next week," Minnie said as we parted.

Our weekly meeting was a constant in our lives. Even while our living arrangements remained unsettled, I was still at Debare's and Minnie was still at Helen's, our friendship remained steadfast.

～

Without income from his illegal weapons business, Dad couldn't pay the mortgage on the family home in Kennison. Rather than let it

go into foreclosure, it was up for sale. As I drove by the house one afternoon an idea popped into my head. I couldn't wait to share it with
Debare and his father later that night.

"After the house sells, can I get the money from the sale, at least
part of it? Shouldn't I be entitled to something? I lost my mother and
my father will spend the rest of his life in prison. If it weren't for you,
I'd be in foster care—or worse—homeless and fending for myself."

"You make a good point, Mia," Debare's father said as he glanced
toward his wife with a pleased smile. "I hope you'll consider studying
the law someday, you've got the aptitude for it."

"I'd like to buy a small place of my own, nothing fancy." I said a bit
hesitantly. It seemed like I was asking for a lot, but it was my future.
I couldn't stay here forever. Debare was going away to college next
year. It would be strange, just me and his parents in this huge house.

"You'll be seventeen in a few months, am I right?" he asked.

"Yes, why?"

You may be eligible to become an emancipated minor. With one
parent who's deceased and one who will likely be incarcerated for a
long time, you might have a case. I'll look into it."

~

The next time Minnie and I got together, I talked non-stop about
the possibility of becoming emancipated and getting a place of my
own. I was already planning what colors to paint the rooms. I'd have
lots of plants, I decided, both inside and out. Oh, and a dog! A dog
to keep Tinker company. I always wanted a dog but Mother said they
were too much work. Cats were low maintenance. That's how I got
Tinker from a shelter. When I finally stopped to take a breath, I realized that Minnie hadn't said a word.

"I'm sorry," I said. "I was so busy going on about my future that I
forgot to ask what's going on with you."

"I hope it works out for you, Mia. I really do." She paused momentarily, collecting her thoughts. "As for me, I'm not sure. I need

to break free from Helen. She thinks because she found me and offered me a place to live that it gives her authority over me. At first, she was against my reaching out to Anna, but now that I have it's like she expects me to move in with her. That's not going to happen. Even if Anna asked me—which she won't—I don't fit into her privileged world. I'd be a fish out of water. To tell the truth, I miss my homeless friends. Life was simpler at the homeless camp, not easier by a longshot, but no responsibilities like opening a checking account, paying my phone bill, doing laundry, helping with meals. It's not that I don't want to do these things, it's just that I'd like to do them in a place of my own." She thought for a moment and asked, "Does that make sense? I figure I'll never be independent if I don't start making my own decisions. God knows I'm not getting any younger."

"It makes perfect sense," I agreed. "I'm trying to do the same thing. I'm thankful to have Debare's parents supporting me, but my goal is to be independent, too, my own person."

"We both have the same dream," Minnie said, "it sounds like you also have a plan."

"I guess you could call it a rough draft," I said, "but it's a start."

~

As I drove around town in Mother's green car I kept an eye out for houses for sale. Most were new and much too big for me. My dream house was a homey cottage with a maple tree in the front yard providing shade in the summer and color in the fall. My needs were simple, two bedrooms and a sunny kitchen.

As the school year dragged on, I slogged through my studies, doing the minimum to pass but nothing more. My goal was to earn enough credits to graduate. College wasn't on my radar. Debare, on the other hand, was an exemplary student, making the honor roll, the star player on the soccer team, and a member of the chess club. It all had to do with getting accepted into a prestigious college. He was so busy I barely saw him. Our relationship began to change. He started treating me like a little sister instead of his girlfriend.

Debare flew to my rescue like a superhero if word reached him that I was being harassed by the mean girls or anyone else. His friends also looked out for me and told him if I received a low grade or didn't turn in an assignment. He became the big brother that I never had. So, which was it—was I Debare's girlfriend—or his little sister?

When he had spare time, which was rare, we talked about soccer, his college applications, who was dating whom, and who had broken up. Debare was my best friend, but I wanted more. Little wonder I was confused. Reason enough for me to put distance between us to sort things out. I longed for Debare to be my boyfriend again, not my big brother.

I wondered if his parents thought that we would eventually get married. Were they grooming me to be their daughter-in-law? It wasn't something I could ask them outright and I didn't want to seem ungrateful for their generosity. But their sheltering me didn't guarantee them a daughter-in-law.

~

As a little girl I'd read all the Little House books by Laura Ingalls Wilder. They fascinated me because they were set in a time that was simpler in some ways and more challenging in others. It was a struggle to survive in the wilderness with endless work and constant worry about the crops, weather, and predators like bears and wolves. But it also meant sitting by a cozy fire, snuggling under a feather comforter, baking bread and listening to Pa play the fiddle. I imagined myself living in a log house in the woods, a horse and some chickens scratching around a yard with a clothesline and a picnic table. It was a fantasy, I knew, but I wasn't about to give up on my dream. One thing was certain, there were no such houses in Kennison. I would have to search beyond the city limits and then some.

After spending hours searching for my dream house with Margo, a real estate agent and friend of the Adebayo's, I was about to give up. With her dyed blond hair and heavy make-up, Margo was the only person I knew who still smoked. She always kept the window open when we were in the car. I knew she was helping me as a favor to the Adebayo's but she was rapidly losing patience with my dream of a log cabin. In a final effort we drove about twenty miles outside Kennison to the site of a former farming community established by European immigrants ages ago. The gravel road leading up to the dilapidated cabin was overgrown and riddled with potholes. Margo swerved to avoid the worst postholes while low-hanging branches scraped the windshield. Margo stopped the car. "I'm not sure about this. Should we turn back?"

"Let's at least see what's at the end of the road." I said, straining to see through the canopy of branches.

Suddenly, the sun poked through the branches and there, nestled in a grove of oak trees, stood a dilapidated log cabin. Moss carpeted the partially collapsed roof, brambles and vines grew up the decaying logs and through broken windows. Margo and I sat silently for a few moments, taking it all in before I bounded out of the car and pushed through the rough-hewn door hanging by a single hinge. The place was a disaster, but I imagined a cozy armchair in front of the stone fireplace, a rustic table with a vase of wildflowers on the table, a vegetable garden and so much more. As I stood there, mice scurried into hidey holes and birds fluttered to their nests in the rafters. I felt like Cinderella in the attic!

"Watch out for that rotten floorboard," Margo warned. "Have you seen enough? Let's get out of here. This place gives me the creeps!"

"No. Wait. I love it!" I announced, exploring the two tiny bedrooms with tattered curtains instead of doors and lifting the creaky handle on the kitchen water pump.

"You're joking, right?" Margo was incredulous.

"Not at all," I replied. "I can turn this into my dream house, a sanctuary from everything I've been through."

"You realize it would cost thousands to get it livable and up to code."

She was right, of course. The cabin and land were dirt cheap. I would need to use the money from the sale of the Kennison house to replace the roof and floors, get rid of the critters, install a furnace and new windows, indoor plumbing, rebuild the fireplace and so many other projects. It was truly daunting but thrilling!

Buying the dilapidated log house and fixing it up became my mission. I didn't know what would happen after Debare left for college, but I couldn't sit around waiting. Who knew what the future held? Who could have foreseen a year ago the situation I found myself in—homeless and little more than an orphan. Technically not an orphan, but I may as well be. Dad couldn't help me from prison and I wouldn't accept his help anyhow. *He* was the reason my life was turned upside down.

It took months to finalize the sale of the Kennison house and purchase of the log house. Finding the owners of the long-abandoned house in the woods meant searching through archives and old records. Selling the house in Kennison was no easy task, either. Mother's murder there had to be disclosed which was an automatic 'no way' for most house hunters. Word gets around about these things. As a result, Father had to keep lowering the price until a family who didn't believe in ghosts or an afterlife agreed to buy it for less than it was worth.

Before the cabin was officially mine, I visited often, staking out the garden and sketching interior renovations. I scoured DIY web sites for renovating old houses. Tinker became my official mouse catcher. I put her to work during our visits, gasping in horror the first time she laid a dead mouse at my feet. I picked up the lifeless critter by the tail and threw it out the door! Tinker proudly laid each new catch at my feet then waited patiently while I opened her treat jar rewarding her for a job well done. As she munched, I'd hastily throw the carcasses on the site of the planned vegetable garden.

It was springtime before I closed on the cabin. Mr. Adebayo represented me. Debare was there, too. We went out for lunch afterwards to celebrate. Mr. Adebayo raised his glass of iced tea. It was a dual celebration, closing on my cabin in the woods and mine and Debare's graduation from Jane Addams, Debare with high honors and me squeaking by. I was done with that chapter of my life and eager to move on.

"Here's to graduation and Mia's new home!" Mr. A said. We clinked glasses. Now it was my turn.

"I can't tell you how much it means to me to have you on my side. You are my family now and are always welcome in my little house in the woods." I smiled and wiped away a happy tear. "I have one more favor to ask, that I can continue to stay at your house until mine is ready to move in."

Debare's dad nodded in agreement. "Of course, Mia. You are always welcome in our home."

I had so many plans. I needed to prioritize my 'to-do list.' First, of course, the roof had to be replaced and the floors repaired. Indoor plumbing was a necessity. As was fresh chinking on the logs. The fireplace and chimney needed cleaning and tuckpointing.

That summer was exhausting but with a sense of accomplishment with each task completed. Debare helped with the heavy lifting—clearing brush, painting, rototilling the garden. Before the indoor plumbing was installed, we bathed in a metal tub that we filled with buckets of well water left to warm in the sun all day. Two sweaty, grimy bodies exposed to the sun and sky soaked and splashed like little kids. We didn't have to worry about getting water on the bathroom floor, though. We wrapped towels around our tanned bodies and raced into the house, collapsing onto the bed, a wrought iron flee market find.

"Let's just stay in bed until morning," Debare pleaded.

"Are you kidding? I'm starving," I laughed, quickly pulling on cut-offs and a t-shirt. I prepared a meal with whatever staples I had on hand. A salad of wild dandelion greens with beans, rice and sauteed vegetables for the main course.

A young entrepreneur bought the long-abandoned town and began rebuilding the shops on the former Main Street, turning them into artist studios, galleries and boutiques. Trendy coffee shops, eateries and small breweries got wind of the low rents and began migrating to the area. The town was becoming a destination for artisans and entrepreneurs looking for community. The new residents, me included, voted to rename the town Resurrection, for obvious reasons. I felt reborn as well. I had a purpose, a reason to get up every morning. Debare and I became closer as we worked side by side fixing up the house. I stopped thinking of him as a big brother and he didn't treat me like a little sister anymore. He said he respected my effort to move beyond the past and build a new life, just as I had with the cabin.

Planting the garden was our favorite project. First, we sketched out where the corn, green beans, tomatoes, squash and other crops would grow best. Debare broke up the clumps of soil remaining after he rototilled, quite a strenuous job, plowing thick roots of native grasses. I raked neat rows and planted the seeds, marking the rows with empty seed packets staked into the ground like I'd seen in gardening magazines. I imagined us dressed as homesteading farmers, me in a sunbonnet and calico dress just like Laura Ingalls, and Debare in breeches, a muslin shirt and a floppy straw hat like Pa's.

One sunny afternoon, my hair slicked back with sweat, Debare showed me a rusty horseshoe he'd found in the dirt. He brushed off the dirt and polished it with a wire brush. We rushed inside to hang it above the door. Afterwards we stepped back and admired our handiwork. "It's good luck when the opening points up," I said.

Debare smiled his killer smile, "I think your luck is definitely looking up."

The 'little house,' as we called it now, was our sanctuary. We were safe, disconnected from the violence of the world beyond Resurrection. We were playing house and we knew it, but while we were together we refused to let anything ruin our happiness.

At the height of summer, the garden exploded with green beans and the sweetest tomatoes I had ever tasted. I always sent Debare home with a bag full of vegetables: peppers, tomatoes, green beans. The pumpkins grew bigger and rounder by the day. We tried to avoid talking about Debare leaving for school. But as the days grew shorter and the nights cooler, I had to face reality. Debare was leaving and I wouldn't see him until Thanksgiving.

I prepared a farewell dinner of corn-on-the cob and burgers on the outdoor grill. I incorporated fresh ingredients from the garden, freshly picked green beans and lettuce. We finished a bottle of red wine that Debare had brought from home and spent the rest of the evening sitting by the fire, enjoying our time together before he left for school. I hated to say good-bye, but I would never stop him from following his dream as I had followed mine.

Debare promised to remain faithful to me while he was away at school and I loved him for it. But I also knew that such pledges were difficult to keep and would only result in guilt and tears.

"I love you, Debare. You were my first love. But I won't hold you to a promise that will be difficult, if not impossible for both of us to keep. I don't want to lose you, but I won't tie you down, either." It was a tearful farewell. I watched him drive away and went inside and cried until Tinker, concerned, curled up next to me.

During the day I was busy with cabin chores and gardening. I researched canning vegetables and ended up with shelves of beans, tomatoes and beets. I didn't think about Debare when I was busy puttering about. But in the evening when the sky faded from pink to mauve to purple, I couldn't help thinking about him away at school, making new friends, going to parties and settling into campus life. I tried to focus on our time together and anticipate our Thanksgiving reunion. We talked on the phone, but it wasn't the same as having him here with me. We never were ones for long phone conversations. We were busy people, me with my little house and Debare with his studies. He was always a serious student. His parents had high expectations for him, as did he.

The Adebeyo's invited me for Thanksgiving dinner while I counted the days until I held Debare in my arms again. I brought the last of the tomatoes from the garden and whatever else I could salvage before the frost settled in. It was a joyful reunion and after helping clear the table, load the dishwasher, and scrub the pots and pans, Debare and I retreated upstairs.

We listened to music and talked, Debare about school and I explained about putting the garden to bed for the winter. It wasn't long before we stopped talking, shed our clothes and held each other close, as I had imagined. It had been months since we make love, but we took our time not sprinting to the finish line. Debare was attentive to my needs. Was someone coaching him, teaching him the finer points of lovemaking? I didn't ask, but the thought of him in bed with someone else made me crazy with jealousy. But his new skills paid off. For the first time I experienced an explosive release that left me breathless. So that's what it was all about, I thought, before drifting off the sleep with Debare cradling me in his arms.

~

Minnie liked her job at the library. When a long-time library employee retired, Minnie began working full-time. The pay wasn't great, barely enough to rent a one-bedroom subsidized apartment, but Minnie enjoyed her job. Her duties included restacking returned books, setting up seasonal displays, culling worn or damaged books from the shelves, orienting new patrons and greeting the regulars. She continued honing her computer skills thanks to Roberta.

On more than one occasion I reminded Minnie that I had an extra bedroom in my cabin. Would Minnie consider moving in with me?

"I'm grateful for your invitation, Mia, but I love my independence and my cozy apartment. I've learned to appreciate the solitude of living on my own, especially after the chaos of the homeless camp. Little things that others take for granted are a delight, like enjoying morning coffee in the kitchen while the sun washes over me. Helen always kept her house too warm for me. Now I can set the thermostat to my liking or open a window if I'm too warm. I appreciate your offer, but I'm happy where I'm at. Besides, I'd have to give up my library position. How would I get back and forth with no bus service?" She had a point.

"Any news from Anna?" I knew that their relationship was rocky, but on the plus side, Minnie and Victoria were friends now, so Minnie got news about Anna through her.

"Victoria dropped a bombshell the other day. Turns out I have a granddaughter! Her name is Alicia. She attends boarding school in France. Of course, Anna wants her to have nothing to do with me. I don't think Alicia even knows that I exist. With Victoria's help I'm going to contact her when she turns eighteen, outside Anna's control."

"If you need help, I know a good lawyer," I smiled and sipped my chamomile tea.

~

I basked in the golden warmth of Indian summer, but inevitably the days turned rainy and cold. Minnie and I sipped hot chocolate and spiced tea at our weekly get together. I was invited to the Adebayo's for Christmas, so I asked Minnie over for a pre-Christmas dinner at the cabin. She had already made other plans, however. Victoria invited her to stay at the house for the holidays. Minnie was thrilled and asked me to help her shop for a holiday outfit and gifts for Anna, Victoria, and the granddaughter she had yet to meet.

I needed a new outfit as well. Minnie and I made a day of clothes shopping. I persuaded her to try something new, outside her comfort zone. We laughed at ourselves wearing outrageous outfits like bedazzled leggings paired with off-the-shoulder tops. Then we got down to business and searched for outfits we would wear. I chose a flowing skirt, a V-neck sweater, a silk shirt and ballet flats. It was indulgent, but I hadn't spent money on clothes in forever. It was a far cry from my usual outfit of overalls, a man's button-down shirt and work boots.

Minnie chose a navy knit dress cinched at the waist. May as well show off her slender figure, right? It fit her perfectly. I selected a rhinestone-studded silver belt to add some holiday sparkle. We parted in anticipation of the upcoming holiday, knowing that we'd share stories when we returned.

I arrived early at the Adebayo's to help his mother prepare dinner of roast beef, baked potatoes, and vegetables, including pounded yams and jollof rice, traditional Nigerian dishes. The textures and spicy flavors livened up the holiday fare. Debare hadn't arrived home from school yet. The Adebayo's and I sat in the living room talking and sipping wine. They were okay with letting Debare and I drink wine or beer at their home. I talked about how homey and comfortable my little house was and invited them for a visit. Mr. A talked about the case against Marco and assured me that my father was cooperating with the feds, which would result in a reduced sentence. Dinner was ready and still no Debare. When he finally bounded in the door. He wasn't alone. He hadn't told anyone he was bringing a guest.

"Everyone, this is my friend Kirsten. She can't go home for Christmas and the campus will be closed, so I invited her. I hope that was alright." Alright or not, here was beautiful blonde Kirsten in the living room.

An awkward silence hung over the gathering. It was too late for me to fake a sudden migraine or stomach upset. I had planned on just Debare and me for the holidays. True to form, Debare's parents welcomed her warmly. I tried to follow their lead, but it was difficult to put on a happy face while feeling jealous and suspicious of this Kirsten person.

"Everything smells delicious. Let's eat. I'm starving!" Debare insisted and not a moment too soon. I had no idea what to say to Kirsten—or Debare, for that matter.

I listened while Debare and Kirsten talked about their classes and campus life. At a lull in the conversation I mentioned the abundant harvest I'd had and preparing the garden for winter by weeding and adding mulch to the soil. "The pickled beets are from my garden," I announced.

My holiday plans with Debare now included a third person, not exactly what I had in mind for quiet evenings in the little house, snuggling in front of the fire with mugs of cocoa, but I had no choice. If I wanted to spend time with Debare I had to include Kirsten.

Turns out she was enthralled with my rustic cabin. In her perfect English and lilting accent, she shared stories about her ancestors living on the land raising sheep and goats. Although I was cool to her at first, it was hard not to like her. She was beautiful and charming and I was more than a little jealous. I made it clear that Debare and I had history together, lots of history. I was determined to be a good host and included her in the festivities. Mother would have been proud. Although Christmas was officially over, we donned hoodies, mittens and boots and hiked into the woods to cut down a small pine tree. We spent the evening decorating it with strands of popcorn, cranberries and paper chains. We devoured half the popcorn, washed down with hot coco and marshmallows.

Sleeping arrangements on their first night were a bit awkward. I managed to get Kirsten alone and explained that Debare and I always slept together in my room.

"Of course," Kirsten said, smiling. "I understand perfectly." I'd made up the bed in the extra room with an antique quilt I'd bought in town and fresh matching sheets. We said goodnight and headed to our rooms. It was a joyful reunion for Debare and I. We tried to keep the noise down out of respect for Kirsten, but now it was her turn to be jealous.

The night before she and Debare left I was determined to have private time with Debare. I asked him to accompany me into town for snacks and egg nogg while Kirsten prepared knack, Swedish Christmas toffee.

We began making out in the car and one thing led to another. It felt secretive and forbidden, which only heightened the sexual tension. I told Debare again that I loved him reminding him that he was my first and only love. It was the last time I'd see him for months. I finally acknowledged the elephant in the room, "What about Kristen? Are you two…what are you to each other, exactly?" There. I'd said it. It was out in the open.

"We're just friends. Honestly, I felt sorry for her being so far from home at Christmas. She has a serious boyfriend in Sweden."

"Damn. Sometimes I wish you weren't such a good person! Just know that I won't lose you without a fight—and it won't be pretty!" I kissed him again and snuggled before I zipped my jeans, raked my fingers through my hair, and we went inside. My silly grin, touching Debare's arm, lingering next to him in the kitchen said it all; we were still a couple. Kirsten smiled perceptively as she served the toffee with mugs of hot coffee.

~

I arrived at our usual time for coffee with Minnie, eager to tell her about Christmas with Debare's family and his surprise guest. I sipped a latte and waited…and waited some more. No Minnie. She couldn't possibly have forgotten. I was concerned, but not panicked. When I called her cell it went directly to voice mail, not like Minnie at all. I tried texting and calling. No word from Minnie.

Two days passed. Now I was panicking. Each message was more urgent until Minnie's mailbox was full. I showed up at her apartment.

Nobody came to the door. I went to the library and talked to her friend Rosemary.

"As far as I know she's still at her daughter's house. Sorry I can't be more help."

The following week I returned to the coffee shop. Again, no Minnie. It was time to call the police. Before I called to alert the authorities, I called Minnie's number one more time. A breathless Minnie answered. I broke down in tears, I was so relieved.

"I'm so sorry Mia. I just figured out how to listen to my messages! I'm sorry you were worried." In hurried, choppy sentences Minnie explained that her granddaughter, Alicia, arrived home from boarding school for the holidays. She hadn't been feeling well for quite a while. The local physician couldn't figure out what was wrong. After Christmas Anna had her undergo a complete physical with countless tests.

"What is it? Is she alright?" I asked, caught off guard by this new development.

"It's not good. Anna's ex-husband has a history of kidney disease. Alicia has inherited it. Her diet is severely restricted and it looks like she'll either need to undergo dialysis several times a week or find a kidney donor."

"Oh," I whispered. "I'm so sorry."

"The good news is that I might be a match. I'm undergoing tests now."

"What about Anna? Couldn't she donate a kidney to her only child?" Of course, Anna would be the first choice. Why is Minnie even considering donating her kidney?

"I didn't know it, but Anna developed Type One diabetes when she was a child. She takes daily insulin shots. It disqualifies her from donating."

The pieces were falling into place. Minnie wasn't good enough for Anna's daughter until she needed a new kidney. Now, Minnie's kidney might end up saving Alicia's life.

"When will you be coming home to Kennison? I miss you."

"If I'm a match I won't be home for a while. If I'm not, I'll be home soon."

There it was. Minnie had the grandchild she'd longed for and as a bonus she might have the opportunity to save her life. How could Anna reject her now?

Knowing Minnie as I did, I knew she wouldn't hesitate to undergo the painful procedure no matter the physical cost to herself. Minnie and I were like family, but Alicia was the real thing. Minnie's news underscored the undeniable truth that family is everything. Maybe it was time for me to rebuild my relationship with Emma, my only connection to my surviving parent.

I kept procrastinating calling Emma. What to say? It was sure to be awkward. I hadn't spoken to Emma or my father since I rushed from the room after he announced that she was pregnant and that they were getting married. Finally, I got up the courage to call.

"Emma? It's Mia."

Silence, then, "Mia. Hello. I didn't expect to hear from you," Emma replied guardedly.

"I'm sorry I stormed out of the room that night at Debare's. I wasn't ready for the news about you and Dad. But he's still my father and you're still…honestly, I'm not sure what you are to me now."

"Dick and I got married by a justice of the peace at the jail where he's being held awaiting trial. Technically, that makes me your stepmother."

"Oh. Well, congratulations, I guess." After a few awkward moments, "It's just too weird. We used to be friends and now you're my stepmother. It's hard to process."

In the background I heard a squalling infant.

"Mia, I have to go. David just woke up and as you can hear, he's starving! I'm so glad you called. Talk later?"

So, I had a little brother, a stepbrother named David. Another bombshell. I few days later, Emma called back. We agreed to meet at her apartment. I brought carry-out food and a bouquet of roses.

Emma answered the door wearing a black tunic and leggings, her red hair in a ponytail.

"Thanks for the flowers. Let me put them in water."

"Where is my little brother?"

"Thank God he's asleep. Being a new mom is exhausting. I never knew what sleep deprivation felt like until now. Plus, I haven't been out of the house except to shop for groceries with Davey in his infant carrier. I've lost contact with the outside world."

"Sounds grim. Not exactly two thumbs up for motherhood."

"Don't get me wrong, I love him to pieces, but it's hard, especially with your dad in jail awaiting trial."

"How long will he nap?"

"This is his long nap. He just went down before you came so he should stay sleeping for a couple of hours,"

"Why don't you get out of the house, alone, for a while. I can babysit."

"Are you sure? Have you ever babysat an infant?"

"No, but how hard can it be? Especially if he's asleep. I know you're supposed to support his head and burp him after a bottle."

"Mia, you're a God send. I love you!" She hugged me and kissed my cheek.

"The clock is ticking. Get the heck out of here before he wakes up. Have fun!"

After Emma left, I crept into the bedroom. Swaddled in blue from his knit cap to his sleeper lay my baby brother, his chest gently rising and falling. He had chubby cheeks, pink lips and a porcelain complexion. Would he be a ginger like his mother and his aunt? If Natalie were alive, Davey would be her nephew. We'd be family!

My afternoon visit turned into several days. I felt sorry for Emma, completely alone with a newborn. When I asked about her parents, she said they couldn't accept that she got pregnant out of wedlock to a criminal! I was her only lifeline. I slept on the sofa and handed Davey to Emma for feedings when he fussed during the night. I schlepped the never-ending sheets, sleepers, burp cloths and stained maternity tops to the laundry room. Emma was right, it was exhausting, but I formed a bond with little Davey while I held him when he fussed, burped him and changed his diaper. If I ever became a mother, it would be hands-on training, although parenthood wasn't on my radar.

Emma thanked me repeatedly for my help, but I knew if I stayed much longer, I might be tempted to stay indefinitely. I had my own life to live. My chickens needed attention. It was time to start planning the garden and ordering seeds. I couldn't leave Emma without a safety net, though. Without Emma knowing, I called her parents. I told them that no matter how they felt about the baby and Emma's marriage to Dick, she needed their help. She was their daughter. And Davey was their grandchild.

Now it was time to get back to my routine at the little house. The chickens were ravenous. Tinker was a bit distant at first but came around when I offered treats and cleaned her litter box.

Nestled in an overstuffed chair by the fireplace one evening, I thought about the latest events in my ever-changing life. Father was in jail awaiting trial. Emma had her baby and needed a lot of support. And Debare? I missed him. I missed the smell of him and his smooth, muscular body, but mostly his soft lips. But he was away at school, studying, playing soccer and, I assumed, dating other people. I needed to get out of the house and explore the tiny village of Resurrection, take a ceramics class, and make some new friends. My thoughts turned to Minnie. Turns out she was a match and had undergone surgery to donate her kidney to Alicia. I'd sent cards, letters and flowers, but we hadn't spoken in a while. I dialed her number.

"Hello?" Her voice was a whisper.

"Minnie? Is that you?" I held my breath, straining to hear. "It's Mia. I'm so sorry. It sounds like I woke you. I can call back." I said although I really wanted to talk to her.

"No. it's alright. I wasn't sleeping. It's just that reaching for the phone is…well I'm not going to lie, it's painful."

"Oh Minnie. I'm so sorry I didn't come to visit. Are you still in the hospital? Is anyone there with you?"

"When Victoria's not with Alicia, she's here with me. Anna's been in. She's mostly with Alicia, though."

"How's Alicia doing?"

"Alicia's doing as well as can be expected, the doctors tell me. We're both in pain. They told us it would be painful, but nothing prepares you for it. The drugs help, but they wear off before you're due for another dose."

"I'm so proud of you, Minnie, giving your kidney to someone you'd just met, even if she is your granddaughter. Especially after Anna has been so mean to you. You are a saint."

"Ha! I'm no saint. I did what I felt I had to do to save my granddaughter's life," Minnie said. "I'm pretty sure you would have done the same thing in my shoes."

"I'd like to think so, but who knows? Guess what? I'm a big sister!" I told Minnie about the time I spent helping Emma with Davey.

"I'm so proud of you, Mia. You really are turning out to be quite a young woman."

Minnie's recovery took longer than expected. Alicia was home planning to attend college stateside while Minnie remained at the hospital struggling to regain her strength. She walked the halls with a walker during the day and had physical therapy several times a week. As her discharge date approached, she wasn't strong enough to make the trip to Kennison or to care for herself without help.

"Minnie, I'm coming out there to care for you. You shouldn't be by yourself," I insisted.

"Don't worry. I'm here at Anna's house. Victoria is hovering over me like a mother hen. She's been so kind and generous. I do miss the library and Roberta, though."

"Well, as soon as you're strong enough to travel you'll come and stay with me for a while. There aren't any stairs in the little house, and I have an extra bedroom."

~

According to Minnie, Anna's house had every creature comfort and modern convenience including an elevator. What it lacked was fresh air and the coziness of a country cottage. When Minnie was strong enough to travel, I took her to my little house where she could regain her strength.

A gentle breeze ruffled Minnie's hair while we sat on the porch one afternoon. The stress of the surgery had taken its toll. Minnie's physical and emotional reserves were depleted. She used a cane to maneuver around the house. She barely ate the meals I prepared—hearty soups, roasted vegetables, puddings, muffins. She was in a dark place. I showered her with love and attention, determined to lift her out of her funk. I arranged a cozy nook on the porch where she could relax with a book and a cup of tea. I planted purple and yellow spring pansies in an ancient crock and purchased a wicker chair and footstool from an antique shop and painted it daffodil yellow. I wrapped a multi-colored quilt around her legs. Tinker curled up at Minnie's feet.

I spent mornings working in the garden dressed in my usual outfit—faded overalls, a flannel shirt of Dad's, boots and a pair of gardening gloves. The aroma of newly turned earth was like a tonic, promising new life. In the afternoon, when the sun was the warmest, I'd join Minnie on the porch, her face turned toward the sunlight. She closed her eyes listening to birdsong and buzzing insects. She couldn't identify individual birds by their song but was determined to learn. She wanted to know everything she could about my little corner of the world.

As the days passed Minnie's appetite improved. She got stronger and no longer needed the cane, but she still walked cautiously. When she was feeling up to it, we drove into town for groceries and garden supplies. We spent the afternoon browsing in the shops and had a leisurely cup of tea and a homemade scone at the local café.

As Minnie regained her strength, she became curious about what was happening in the world, especially in Kennison. She mentioned more than once that she missed her job at the library and her friends there, especially Roberta. The director had promised that her job would be waiting for her. Since Resurrection didn't have a library, I arranged for the Kennison Chronicle to be mailed to the house. Reading the Chronicle on the porch in the afternoon became part of our afternoon routine. The days grew longer and warmer. Green shoots poked up through the soil that I had carefully tilled, watered and fertilized.

"Have you seen this?" Minnie asked, sitting upright in her chair. "It says here that an anonymous benefactor has donated two and a half million dollars to build a permanent shelter for the homeless of Kennison, complete with classrooms for job training, a communal kitchen, and laundry facilities. The shelter will replace the encampment at the crumpling viaduct under the interstate. Building is slated to begin within eighteen months."

"That's fantastic! It's exactly what Kennison needs," I said.

"I wonder who the anonymous donor is?" Minnie mused.

~

My vegetable garden was thriving. I brought the produce that Minnie and I couldn't eat to the local farmers' market. As my second summer at the cabin waned, Minnie had fully regained her strength. One muggy evening on the porch as fireflies blinked on and off, Minnie put her glass of iced tea down and reached for my hand. I sensed what Minnie was about to say and despite preparing myself for it, I felt a hiccup of sadness. I loved having Minnie with me. She was the perfect companion—she did her thing, and I did mine. In the evening we came together and talked about our day—two women with their histories of tragedy cobbling together a new life.

"Mia, I love you as if you were my own daughter, more, truth be told. I can never repay you for all the kindness you have shown me." Minnie's eyes glistened. "We knew this day would come. I'm ready to go back to my apartment, my job, and my friends in Kennison."

Tears streamed down my cheeks. I squeezed Minnie's hand.

"And I love you as my own mother, maybe more," I said, laughing and crying at the same time. "This isn't goodbye. It's 'see you later for tea' in Kennison. I'll never let you slip from my life again."

~

Our bond of friendship remained strong, waxing and waning as we explored new paths. I realized that working the soil was my calling. I mastered my own garden and went on to establish a local organic cooperative. I had a lot to learn about organic farming and dove right in, learning from the others in the co-op. My land was my life and while I dated occasionally, usually one of the artists from town, I felt fulfilled. Debare came to visit occasionally and was amazed at what I'd accomplished. I would never stop loving him. I dreaded the day he'd tell me about a serious relationship, but it never came. He applied to graduate school while I was content drawing strength and healing from the land.

Minnie quickly settled back into her life in Kennison. She continued to learn about computers from Roberta and, at her suggestion, began taking classes at the junior college. She realized that she loved learning and made it her life's mission to make up for lost time by earning an associate degree.

She was still reticent to fly so she took the train a few times a year to visit her family. Finally, she insisted that Anna, Alicia and Victoria come to Kennison for a visit. Upon their arrival, Anna wanted to see the site of the new homeless shelter. Construction was well under-way. It was an impressive five-story structure surrounded by a greenway with trees and a community garden plot. Anna took a keen interest in every detail of the project, even conferring with the site manager. While she never admitted it, Minnie was sure that Anna was the anonymous donor who was funding the project. She was so proud of the woman that Anna had become, despite her initial reluctance to accept the circumstances of her adoption.

Minnie was assigned to the periodical section at the library which was a perfect fit because of her keen interest in current events. It was her job to shelve new magazines and newspapers and cull the old editions. A headline in the Kennison Chronicle caught her eye, *Local Social Worker Under Investigation.* She gasped. On the front page above the fold was a photo of Helen Rutherford, much younger, but clearly her. According to the article, the state licensing board was made aware of improprieties in certain adoptions overseen by Ms. Rutherford.

The truth had caught up with Helen. Her misdeeds were exposed, but by whom? Only four people knew about the circumstances of Anna's adoption: Anna, Minnie, Victoria and Mia. Could it have been a former co-worker or another family who finally learned the truth?

The investigation dragged on as these things tend to do. The wheels of justice turn slowly, but they do turn. A year later, Minnie was subpoenaed to testify before the grand jury investigating the matter. She immediately called Anna with the news.

"I'm coming out there. I want to be there for you—for us. That woman affected both our lives, especially yours. We need to make sure this never happens again. No one should have to go through what you did, Mom."

Minnie's heart skipped a beat. She couldn't have held back her tears even if she'd wanted.

"Mom, what's wrong? Are you okay? Was it something I said?"

"Yes, it was. Do you realize that you called me *Mom?* I love you, Anna. I'll see you soon."

~

Before the news of the investigation broke, Helen's colleagues had planned a party to celebrate her thirty years of service in the community. After the news broke Helen requested that the party be cancelled. She became reclusive, refusing to talk about the matter to friends, coworkers, and especially journalists who frequently called and knocked on her door.

Months later, Minnie went to see her. When Helen answered the door, the color drained from her face. She leaned against the doorframe for support.

"Minnie," Helen whispered. She stood silently for a long time. Finally, she spoke.

"Apologies could never erase what I did to you…to your family. I'm so sorry. I tried to make it right by finding you and giving you a home, but…"

Minnie cut her off in mid-sentence. "I accept your apology, but that's not why I'm here."

"Just so you know," Helen said, "I've lost everything—my career, my colleagues, my standing in the community. I may even lose my pension." Helen had aged since Minnie last saw her. Her skin was sallow and she had wrinkles where there had once been laugh lines.

"I don't want anything from you. I came here to tell you that…" Minnie hesitated.

The two women stared unblinkingly at each other. Helen wondered how Minnie intended to extract revenge for her misdeeds, which she knew were great. Would Minnie bring a civil suit against her, demand money? Anything was possible.

"I wanted to tell you that I forgive you," Minnie said softly. "Truly, I can't move forward with my new life until I put the old one behind me."

Helen sobbed into her hands. It would have been easier if Minnie had unleashed an angry tirade. She could deal with that, not Minnie's forgiveness. She stiffly hugged Minnie and stepped back. "I don't deserve your forgiveness. Please, come inside."

Minnie shook her head and simply said, "Goodbye Helen. I wish you well," and turned to leave. Helen watched her go and quietly closed the door.

~

It was mid-summer. Cicadas were buzzing nonstop, and the air was still. The sun was blazing as I bent, weeding the garden wearing only overalls with a sports bra and a straw hat. I stood up to wipe the sweat from my eyes and immediately felt light-headed. I blinked and looked at the gravel road leading to the house. Walking toward me, backlit by the hazy sun, were two figures. I was in a trance as I watched them approach. As they got closer, I recognized two women. Mother smiled serenely holding out her arms to me. Natalie waved, her red hair forming a halo that highlighted her freckles. I took a few steps then began running toward them, calling their names. As I got closer, the apparition began to fade, but an overwhelming feeling of peace and love enveloped me. Mother and Natalie disappeared into the blinding sunlight. I smiled. Tears trickled down my cheeks. I couldn't wait to tell Minnie.

About the Author

Kathleen McElligott's work appears in numerous anthologies and websites. She is a member of The Society of Midland Authors and The Chicago Writers Association. She has read her work at Chicago's Printers Row Lit Fest and other Chicago venues. She enjoys hiking in the Southwest and is an avid bicycle tourist, most recently along the Danube River. She lives outside Chicago with her long-time partner.

She wrote about her experiences as a school nurse in her first book, *Mommy Machine* (Heliotrope Press, 2008). Her second book, *1638 East Palace* (Adelaide Books, 2019), is the sequel and continues Elaine and Christa's story. Both books are about sisterhood and will be re-released in 2025.

www.ingramcontent.com/pod-product-compliance
Lightning Source LLC
Chambersburg PA
CBHW060449300726
48975CB00008B/2449